Ta

Alt Vegas: Visitations

Edited by: Notch Publishing House
Fiction by:
Wren Cavanagh
Stephanie Hoogstad
Shivangi Narain
Wade Newhouse
Henry Snider
Josh Snider
Junior Sokolov

Copyright notice

Disclaimer

This is a work of fiction. All the names, characters, businesses, places, events, and incidents in this book are either the product of the author's imagination or used in a fictitious manner. Any resemblance to actual persons, living or dead, or actual events is purely coincidental.

Dedication

To Henry Snider, who pushed and shoved this one over the finish line. This anthology wouldn't have seen the light of day without his help and energy.

Introduction

The world we know is held together by delicate strands—air, water, soil, warmth—all carefully balanced in a symphony of life. For millennia, these elements have nurtured humanity, teaching us the patterns of seasons and the rise and fall of life. Yet, as nature shifts, reshaped by forces seen and unseen, what was once familiar begins to twist into something alien.

In this anthology, each story explores a world in flux. As climates shift and ecosystems adapt in unpredictable ways, people find themselves in landscapes they barely recognize. Technology, desperation, and resilience drive them to confront the unfamiliar and navigate environments that challenge not only their physical survival but also their sense of place and purpose.

These tales offer a glimpse into lives disrupted and remade by bizarre transformations. From unexpected encounters with evolving ecosystems to moments of quiet tension as people reckon with their surroundings, each story examines the thin line between adaptation and unease. Here, the natural world takes center stage—not as an enemy, but as a powerful force that reshapes everything in its path, including us.

So, step into these pages and explore a future shaped by changing lands, skies, and seas. In these stories, our environment is both familiar and strange, a reminder of how deeply we are bound to the world—and how quickly that bond can be tested. Step into this collection of stories and witness the raw, unpredictable face of a world forever altered.

Hold your breath. Change calls, and it does not wait.

Get me out

Wren Cavanagh

On the 5th of July Shaya Holt gets her father's phone call before the sun even hinted at its daily return at the horizon's edge. Being summer, that made it damn early in the morning.

"Come and get me out of here. People are dying and the cops aren't showing up!"

She wipes the sleep from her face, feeling simultaneously groggy, and jolted. "Okay wait, what? What do you mean? What's going on?"

"Something attacked the facility, wild animals..." he stammers, "a...creatures. It's just a mess. I've got people hiding in my room. 911 said to wait, and when I tried to call them again, they put me on hold. We need to get out now. I think Eunice had a small stroke. And Jim, his heart can get tricky."

"Ok, Hang tight, on the way."

"Don't come alone!"

She ends the call and stumbles out of bed, hopping in the nearest pair of shorts before grabbing a bra and pulling on a t-shirt. She doesn't know what's going on, but her father has his wits about him. He is at the retirement facility for rehab after a fall from a horse broke a hip and leg bones in more places than one would have thought possible. And yet the call makes no sense. Creatures, 911 not responding? Did he have a stroke?

She grabs her car keys while simultaneously dialing the main line for the assisted living, slash, rehab facility and stumbling outside where the cool fresh summer air is both balm and caress. Her dog follows along, wagging his tail as her call goes to voice mail.

"Not good," she mutters and tries 911, but a recording tells her to wait on the line. Instead, she ends the call and pulls up a local news stream on the smartphone. Utterly baffled she reads post after post, updated after update, of fires and fights that went on during the night. And reports of unspecified animal attacks.

Wow, the 4th of July was wild. Deaths, fires...creatures. She calls the facility again, hoping someone will answer and provide a return to normalcy, to sanity. But the reply offers no reassurance.

"Leave a message." *What the hell, really?*

The dog begins to bark at the nearby woods. Great, the neighbors will just love her. "Shut up Tostito! I mean it!" She hisses and swats the dog's butt.

He's been doing that for a few days now, barking at the woods, yet not a squirrel in sight. She slaps her hands to get the dog's attention. "Tostito, c'mon boy. We're leaving. Truck."

The yellow, brown Australian Shepard-some-other-dog mix looks up at her, puzzled at her lack of interest. His woof is interrupted when she grabs him by the collar, places a hand on his rump and shoves him in the truck.

"Dog, it's too damn early for this shit. Shut up."

He lets out a muffled woof as if too polite to openly disagree and resumes his anxious watch of the woods facing the housing complex. Now that she thinks about it, the last time she visited her dad at the assisted living, he was acting as weird as Tostito—sans barking—studying the woods outside the facility. The early morning light reveals the aftermath of out-of-control fires, and the smell of the smoke wafts through the truck's windows. The early morning light illuminates the aftermath of too many fires, and she smells smoke and something else she can't identify wafting through the truck's windows. And along the way, she sees:

Vehicles abandoned on the side of the roads, some with doors shoved wide open as if their passengers had escaped into the night.

Onlookers whose shocked and anxious faces remind her of displaced refugees from distant countries. They stare openly at her as she drives past them.

Brambles, some as large as cars, that seem to move against the wind—but there is no wind, a light breeze is all.

"What the hell, just...what the hell."

The dog sighs.

***

Fifteen minutes and she's past the city limit and into the countryside at Silver Pines, the silver refuge for the silver set. Brambles again, and they are running roughshod about the parking lot and landscape around the facility. Their normal landscaping is dull and uninspired with its green lawns and the nearly unkillable laurels hedges, but at least they had kept it up. She parks and rolls down the windows enough for the dog to be comfortable.

"I'll be right back, you mutt. Behave yourself."

And yet, she remains in the driver's seat with her hand on the handle, staring at the facility. She then scans the parking lot. Yeah, it's early, but the stillness feels out of place. There must be a perfectly reasonable solution to her father's call. Tostito let out a soft growl. She wipes the sweat from her face. The breeze outside would feel nice, and yet she waits. Something is off. At the far end of the parking lot brambles have grown inside an old Ford Taurus, and that...is definitely odd. Had the car been abandoned there, and she hadn't noticed it on her previous visits? Very possible. Its windows seemed filthy with swirls of mud. *But it hasn't rained for weeks, and why is my ass still in this car?*

"Okay, doggo. The window's rolled down, you got fresh air, it's early, and I'll be right back, Behave."

Tostito tries to sneak after her, but she blocks his escape attempt and pushes him back in the passenger's seat.

"Not a day goes by without you reminding that you flunked your obedience classes. Stay put, you mutt!"

She covers the short distance to the main entrance of the assisted living center with a few long strides. Not breaking into a run because she is suddenly far more curious and wary of her surroundings. In the morning stillness, she can hear furtive noises whose origins she can't explain, and those noises grow louder as she nears Silver Pines' main entrance. Its double doors, made of elegant, glossy blond wood with crystal-cut glass insets, are dirtied by smudges and smears.

Shaya first thinks: *This place is slipping.*

And then: *Is that blood? Holy shit, that's blood, and where the hell is everyone? And while we're at it...what the hell happened?*

The lobby area, the main desk, and the immediate hallway are a mess as if the elderly or the feeble residents had gone mad overnight and staged a riot. She feels her blood begin to buzz in her veins and realizes that her breathing got shallow and tight. Shaya sprints for her father's room but only makes it a few feet before a door swing open, and a pair of strong arms lift her off her feet and drag her inside like she'd triggered a human trapdoor spider.

Kicking and cursing she struggles free and almost lands on her ass. Almost, she gets her balance and rears back to wallop her attacker. But with a teeth-bared grimace realizes she knows the grabber. Not only does she know him, but he's one of hers and her dad's favorite people here.

"Elias?!"

Elias Echevarria, a gentle giant of a man, looking ragged and scared. His uniform is bloody and disheveled.

"Shhh." He lifts a finger to his lips and whispers, "Not loud. Shhh."

"Elias, what's going on? Is my dad okay?" She whispers back.

He shakes his head, then gives it a few moments of consideration and shrugs. "Maybe?"

Bewildered Shaya inspects the small vestibule. They are in a waiting room off the main hall where clients meet with nurses or administrators. In the corner furthest from the door, in a commercial and uncomfortable-looking armchair, slumped a glassy-eyed woman. Shaya guesses her for administration or perhaps a volunteer judging by her attire. Informal but still within the professional spectrum. The name tag askance on her vest read 'Kim.'

Kim looks dazed, overwhelmed. She's past welcoming anyone anywhere. Orange dust, or it could be pollen—and hasn't there been a lot of that orange dappling about lately? Whatever it is, it peppers her chest and face. And is that snot? No, it's not snot. Tiny green tendrils poke from Kim's nostrils and almost touch the top of her upper lip. Her eyes and skin have the unhealthy yellow color of someone whose liver is failing badly.

Horrified, Shaya is struck dumb by the other woman's condition, and the worst part is looking into those blue and resigned eyes that stand out against the sick yellow of her corneas. Her heart aches thinking of what the woman must be feeling right now, but there's nothing she can do.

Not my circus, not my monkeys. Get dad out of here, she tells herself. She's no superhero and needs to think of her father first. Shaya turns to leave, but Elias takes her arm in a gentle grasp.

"There's a monster out there. Big."

"I need to get my dad out, and when he called me this morning, he said he had people with him. I thought he'd lost his mind."

She pulls away and pushes the door open, looks up and down the hallway and finds it empty of life, nothing is moving that she can see.

"There's nothing outside. You should be able to get out and get help. Please go, Elias."

***

On the balls of her feet, she jogs down the central hallway, passing the first and second corridors. At the third and final corridor—The main body of the facility would look like an 'E' from the air. She'll take a right that will take her down to her father's room. But it's darker there. And it hits her. The large floor-to-ceiling window at the end of the hallway and the sunroofs that normally brighten the place with natural light are almost obscured by barbaric-looking vines. And in spots, their concentration is so thick daylight can't filter through.

She needs to see this. Whatever this is, it's part of whatever is happening.

The wild thicket on the other side of the glass isn't like any blackberry bush she's seen before. The vines have razor-sharp, almost hook-like thorns at least an inch long and almost bone-like in appearance. The serrated leaves aren't as thick as a succulent's but they still meatier than an average leaf. As Shaya moves closer, the vines writhe, ripple and burst outward, slamming into the glass. She gasps, her muscles tightening with fear as she jumps back. She feels a newfound appreciation for the window separating her from whatever the hell that is. In another aggressive movement, the vines whip against the glass again, revealing a bulbous center she hadn't noticed earlier.

It's got a diameter a bit over a foot with a vertical mouth full of sharp teeth running vertically along its length. Baleful, unfriendly discolorations that might be eyes point back at her. A thin long rasping tongue lashes out and licks the window pane.

It's kinda like a toothy, murderous watermelon octopus hybrid with a grudge.

It's amazing and scary, baffling and enticing, like the colorful sea life that swims behind the thick glass of an aquarium tank. Except this time, Shaya is the one inside the tank, and that thing is outside. And what can she do about it? Not much at all except for staying the fuck away from it.

Not my circus, not my monkeys. Go.

She turns her back on the critter, feeling safe with the glass, brick and mortar barrier keeping it away from her. Still, from a nearby upturned cart, amongst spilled pills, bandages, and assorted medical accouterments, she finds and picks up a pair of scissors. Worst case scenario, she could stab something with it. She looked up at the watermelon gone wrong. In response, it slams its maw at the window as if to say, 'Peekaboo! I see you too!'

THWACK!

The scissors feel puny in her hand just then, but she walks down the corridor. Her father's room is the last one on her left. Silver Pines is a large facility, and there were about a dozen patients rooms on each side of the corridor. Some with doors closed, too many with their doors open. And judging by the breeze that smelled like summer and decay, many residents had kept their windows open. The corridor was a gauntlet, and she had a horrible idea of just what might have crawled through those windows.

"Away from the crowd, fewer people around," he said when he arrived at the facility. "And look, it's got a bigger window."

Good thing he kept the windows closed last night.

Twelve rooms on the left, twelve more on the right. A linen closet on one side, a supply closet on the other, and a couple of other industrial-looking doors. Shaya is glad Tostito remained the truck. Whatever protection the dog might offer would be offset by his utter lack of self-control.

Note to self: obedience class, again.

She passes the first room, its door wide open, and the screen torn from the window's frame lays on the ground with the shreds of the thick commercial drapes. Someone struggled here and bled on the way out. She tightens her grip around the scissors and sidesteps a toppled linen cart. It's commercial sheets and blankets strewn on the floor along with drab medical gowns. Further down, a food cart also lays on its side, and trays of food are spread about the corridor. Ants and flies are already picking away at the spilled food. She walks by two more rooms. From the next room with an open door, a soft rustling sound freezes her mid-step. Her heart is hammering in her chest, and she wonders if whatever is in there can hear it as she moves to the far edge of the hall on the opposite side. From there, she can see that room is full with the murderous things. The vines cover everything but the feet on the bed. Old skinny white feet protruding from under a green hell.

At the door of her father's room, Shaya grabs the handle, it doesn't budge. She pushes her face close to the door, her cheek against the wood and whispers.

"Dad, I'm outside your door."

Muffled sounds, low voices and the sound of furniture being moved away follow.

"Get in here!" He grabs her arm and yanks her in.

***

There is an even dozen of residents, who, with her father, make it a baker's dozen. Thirteen vulnerable people crammed in a small room.

"We need to get you out."

Her dad points to her, "Everyone, this is my daughter. She's great at catching the obvious details."

To their credit, thought Shaya, the other occupants gasped in disapproval. Aghast, one of the women admonishes him with an emphatic whisper. 'David Holt!'

"Okay, okay!" He waves them off, and when he turns to her and grasps her forearm in his strong warm hands. His eyes are sincere and afraid. "I'm sorry, princess. That's Lola. She corrects me a lot. We need two wheelchairs. Emily and Chuck can't walk very well. Rosario is bed-bound, and nobody can manage a sprint from this room."

"Best I can do is a quick shuffle." Admits Chuck.

A soft knock on the door behind her. Then a bark.

"What?!" She knows that bar and yanks the door open.

Tostito and Elias rush in. The big man doesn't beat about the bush. "911 said we need to get out on our own."

"You got through to them, and they aren't coming?" Lola is aghast.

"No help is coming for at least the next two hours. Everyone is busy. We can wait or get out on our own." Elias replies.

"Why's my dog here?!"

"He squeezed out the car window and wouldn't shut up. I let him come with me."

Tostito smiles as only a dog can and squints beatifically up at her.

"Damn it, dog." But pats the scruffy blonde head of the canine rebel.

"I closed the doors to as many of as many rooms along the corridor as I could when I came back in. Not enough, though. I can carry Ms. Emily. And come back for Eunice. And then Rosario."

Shaya looks outside the window. They are on the first floor, and the landscaping outside has raised the ground to near sill level. Still, the area outside looks clear of the murder-melons, razorweeds, killer plants, whatever.

I can come back with the truck and get them out through the window. She thinks, and as if Elias read her mind, he taps her shoulder and then gestures at the door.

"We could walk out with the more able folks, then come back with the truck and load the rest," he says.

She nods, the motley group looks anxious, but they are also nodding their approval.

"It sounds reasonable. Two more days and I would have been discharged, I was dragging my feet because..." Lola glanced at Dave, who winked back at her with a smile. "Never mind. It sounds reasonable."

Dave stands up, his hand on his cane, the other holding a dented and blood-splattered crutch. "Let the gimps and old farts parade begin."

Shaya almost asked where in the hell he'd gotten that crutch. And is Lola his new squeeze? But, priorities.

The first group has six residents, and that includes Elias carrying Emily on his back. The progress was slower than they would have liked. A door to one of the rooms puffed out and back in, and for a few seconds, it froze everyone in their tracks. Then silently, they resumed their journey until they were outside.

***

They placed four people in Elias's suburban but Shaya's dad got in the passenger seat of her truck. "I'll help get them out the window."

"You have been in there a spell, Dad. You're out of shape!"

"She's right, Mr. Holt-"

"Dave. How many times do I have to tell you."

Elias smiled. "Dave, macho. Listen, you sit in the middle if you want. But I'll handle the transport duty. Okay?"

"Fair enough." Her father admitted, and Shaya gave a mental thanks that while brave, her he isn't stupid.

***

She drives her truck over the parking lot curb and finds out that the vines reach and grasp for it as if it held the promise of a tasty treat. *It's made of plastic and metal, you stupid shits!* The vines, or critters, or plants...whatever the hell they are, they aren't strong enough to hold it. But those wicked thorns looked strong enough to punch holes through the tires. And then she hears him.

Wild peals of barking, a streak of gray, black and yellow across the green field announce the arrival of the best dog ever. A mutt powered by the purest canine energy. Tostito, free at last and racing alongside the truck, barking with unbridled enthusiasm.

With bug-eyed shock, Shaya lowers the window to yell at him, and a swipe from a thorny vine narrowly misses her face.

"TOSTITO NO! BACK! GO BACK!"

As if, he ignores her, barking widely and furiously, a courageous canine challenge to all the monsters that be, now and forever. Dancing, barking and baiting them until at last, the vines forsake the truck for him.

In the side-view mirror, she watches those monsters try to hold onto her dog. How she wishes there weren't people to rescue! But she races to her father's old room and stomps on the brakes. With Elias she races to the window where the more able residents are pushing and pulling the large A/C unit to the floor and shoving the window open. In the background, the peals of barking continue. *That dog gets a treat.*

Out came:

Eunice. Whose stroke robbed her of the use of the left arm and leg, slowly makes her way to the window with the help of the other. Elias lifts her up, and Shaya slips her arms under Eunice's shoulders, assisting her to exit through the window. Her face might be a twisted thing, but her eyes are alight with relief.

Janice and Gloria Stoll. Twin sisters to the end. Gloria, the stronger and healthier sister makes it out first and stops to help Shaya pull Janice out before they both go to sit in the back of the truck.

Emily. Already large and heavy has legs whose size and shape make people think of tree trunks, especially if said tree trunks had red, dry and scaly bark. Her heart might want to retire early, but she isn't ready to go yet. Elias and Rosario both walk and push her over the ledge. When she steps over the window frame, she turns and blows a kiss at Rosario.

Rosario. The last one to leave laughs all the way out of the room as Elias pushes him from behind and quickly follows.

"Dad drive." Shays says before jumping in the back of the truck with the Stoll sisters where she claps her hands and yells for her dog.

"TOSTITO! Enough! Come here NOW!"

At last, the dog listens and races toward her. Four feet away from the truck, he sprints for a running leap that defies gravity and lands him into the truck bed to hugs and cheers of victory.

***

Dave looks into the rearview mirror, Elias's car is nowhere to be seen, and neither is it on the street outside Silver Pines. He turns another wide arc avoiding the largest brambles, and gets back on the road to the facility. In the parking lot the suburban made it as far as the exit before hitting the large decorative, carved granite bearing the logo and name of Silver Pines.

Jim is crumpled against the steering wheel. One of his hands clutching at his chest.

Elias gets and pulls Jim's body to the ground before covering him with a blanket from the back of the suburban. From the third floor, a turret-like extension stacked on the corner of the building like a bad idea, a woman waves for their attention from an open window.

"They're everywhere!" she shouts. "I can see them from here. They are everywhere!"

Face Your Fear

Stephanie Hoogstad

Sally awoke from a dreamless sleep on her queen-sized mattress. She rolled out of the left side; the right was already empty. Without any signs of tiredness or enthusiasm, she dressed and brushed her short, curly brunette hair. After putting on her pearls and the final touches of her makeup, she walked down the dimly lit hall. She stared nowhere but straight ahead, ignoring her son's room and the empty nursery.

When she entered the living room, streaks of pinkish-red light trickled in through the curtains. Sally headed to the kitchen and began to gather eggs, bread, butter, bacon, and milk to prepare a hardy breakfast. She did not even notice when her teenaged son, Timmy, came in and sat at the dining table. His coughing fit—so bad that his abnormally small head turned purple—did not disturb her, either. Only when breakfast was ready did she pay him enough attention to lay out a glass of milk, a plate of eggs, toast, and bacon, and some cough syrup. Across from him, she set her own plate, and at the head of the table, she placed some food for her husband.

Sally sat down and ate robotically, and her son followed suit. They finished quickly and took the vile cough syrup without fuss. Timmy then grabbed his backpack, walked around the table, and gave his mother an emotionless hug and kiss while staring at the front door.

As Timmy left the house, Sally picked up the dishes and set them one by one into the sink. When she got to her husband's untouched breakfast, she scraped the food into the trash on top of his dinner from the night before and washed off the remains. She stared into the living room as she worked, her eyes fixed unblinkingly on her wedding picture. Her glazed gaze stayed in front of her as she put the dishes in their assigned spots in the cabinets.

Suddenly, a glass slipped from Sally's grasp and shattered on the floor. Her eye twitched, and her hand curled and uncurled repeatedly. Her breathing grew more rapid. The falling glass played in her mind's eye, again and again. She blinked it away. The calm emptiness returned to her eyes, and Sally resumed her daily chores.

***

Pinkish-red skies greeted Sally as she left her mid-century house. She wore her usual white sundress with a yellow floral pattern, white heels, a white floppy hat, and large, white-framed sunglasses. A matching purse hung lazily from her shoulder. As she walked down the drive and onto the sidewalk, she acknowledged no one. It was as if none of them were there—not Mr. Johnson mowing his lawn; not Ms. Smith walking her chihuahua; not elderly Mrs. Curtis with the tennis-ball-sized lump on her jaw or her four-foot-tall adult grandson as they gimped down the street. Even as Sally passed Mr. Higgins being devoured by a razorweed, she barely looked his way. His own sons did not spare the bloody scene a glance, focused on their soccer game rather than the carnivorous, bush-like creature tearing their father to shreds, knowing that there was no helping him now.

Sally continued her stroll to the market, ignoring the Bel Airs and Thunderbirds on their way to The Strip, where her husband Peter worked as a bartender. Sometimes, she would knock shoulders with someone, but never a word was said. At the market, Sally proceeded with her usual errand of buying milk, eggs, bread, butter, and bacon before leaving once more. She bumped shoulders with the young stock boy Clark, who had a terrible cough, but kept moving. Close behind her, an unfamiliar figure in a pinstripe suit followed.

Like with everyone else, Sally did not pay this figure any heed, and yet the figure followed Sally closely, so closely that Sally could almost feel their presence. Sally continued on her way, reaching a corner two blocks from her house before the figure caught her.

"Excuse me, Mrs. Henderson?" The figure put a hand on Sally's shoulder. Sally only stared at them through her sunglasses. "Your husband wanted me to ask you...what is the date?"

Sally removed her sunglasses, blinking in confusion. "W-what?"

"What is today's date?"

"Oh, that's simple. It's...January 27, 1951..." Sally rubbed her eyes as a headache started to build. "Why would my husband tell you to ask me that? Who are you?"

By the time Sally put her sunglasses back on, the figure was gone. Sally felt her pulse racing. Each breath was rapid and painful. She could suddenly hear...everything. The tires on the asphalt, the horns of the automobiles, the droning monotone voices of the rare conversation...she could hear it all with such volume that her head felt as though it would split in two. And her vision, she could see every color with a vividness that made her eyes water. She clutched at her head and bent over as a coughing fit overtook her. She pulled her hand away from her mouth, and her eyes widened at the sight of deep red blood, deeper than the sky above her. Had the sky always been so unnaturally *red*?

***

"What is the date?" Sally said repeatedly on the walk home. "Why would Peter have someone ask me that?"

The more Sally thought on that question, the greater her headache grew. The air became thick, stifling. She could scarcely breathe. She coughed as hard as Timmy, blood appearing more than once. She was suddenly aware of every sight, sound, and smell, as though she had been asleep her entire life until then. Sally couldn't help but notice all the people walking around her in a zombified state, some sick, some deformed. And yet they all maintained that glassy-eyed stare and rarely acknowledged anyone around them. Had she been like that? For how long?

When she reached her neighborhood, Sally saw Mrs. Curtis and her grandson still slowly making their way down the street while Mr. Johnson mowed his lawn. Ms. Smith had left with her chihuahua, but the Higgins boys still played in their yard. Sally's eyes landed on the lone blackberry bush in front of their house, and a chill ran down her spine. As though it were happening all over again, she saw the razorweed digging its thorns and teeth into Mr. Higgins, ripping skin from muscle and flesh from bone. Blood stained the pristine, well-manicured grass. The light illuminating Mr. Higgins's stare faded. Then, as quickly as it had occurred, the vision disappeared, leaving behind a seemingly ordinary blackberry bush in its place.

***

Sally ate a peanut butter and jelly sandwich at the kitchen counter, listening to the living room clock tick. It was such a hypnotic sound—and one that Sally swore she had never heard before, anywhere. Not in her house, not in friends' houses, not in her parents' house. It was soothing and anxiety-inducing at the same time, confirming her existence while reminding her that *something* was happening. At least it filled the void left by Peter's snoring. As a bartender, he typically worked nights and slept during the day, leaving Sally to listen to the symphony of his snoring while completing her chores. Yet Sally couldn't remember the last time she had heard it.

"'Your husband wanted me to ask you...'" she muttered. She walked to the sink and washed off her plate. "But where is Peter?"

Sally left the plate on the counter and rushed back to her and Peter's bedroom. Like a madwoman, she dug through all their possessions, trying to find some trace of her husband. Nothing in their dressers. Nothing in her vanity. Their closet, his clothes, everything, empty of signs. The only thing missing was his favorite pinstripe suit and fedora, which he wore to work every day. Exacerbated and concerned, Sally fell onto Peter's side of the bed and rested her head on his pillow.

Where was he when she needed him most? Sally's head swam. It was just like when Celia had been born prematurely. Instead of being at the hospital with them, he had gone to the casino to drink until it was his turn to be the bartender. Even Timmy had been there when he wasn't in school...

Then it hit her. Celia. Sweet little Celia, born too small and too soon. The empty nursery just down the hall. Each morning and night, Sally had passed that nursery, but she had not even thought of the little girl she had lost so abruptly. Her heart hurt so deeply just at the thought that she couldn't comprehend that reality. Day in and day out, doing the same thing without any emotion...Tears streamed down her cheeks. She let in a deep breath, then released a loud, primal scream. It ended in a wheezing cough.

After her breath returned to her, Sally stormed to the nursery. It was as though the room were alive. Pink walls with yellow flowers closed in on her. A crib, rocking chair, toy chest, and changing table spun around her. White curtains flared out at her, threatening to strangle her like a pair of lacy boa constrictors. Sally's fists clenched and unclenched, and she shut her eyes tight against her throbbing headache. With another deafening roar, she grabbed the rocking chair and smashed it over the crib. She took a piece of the crib and charged the window, breaking the glass—again and again and again.

A teenaged male scream pierced Sally's ears, snapping her back to the moment. She leaned out the window, avoiding the glass, and found the source of the scream: Timmy being attacked by the razorweed, now the size of the Higgins' Morris Minor.

"Timmy!"

Ignoring the pain, Sally used the piece of crib to widen the hole in the window and climbed through the remaining glass. She tossed her heels as she ran by the front door and dashed across the yard.

As she approached him, only Timmy's torso was still visible. Vine-like tentacles wrapped around him, digging the razorweed's thorns into his skin. One of the tentacles squeezed Timmy's small head so hard that Sally worried it would pop before she reached him.

Sally slid in front of her son and started beating the tentacles with her piece of crib. She pounded mercilessly as they squirmed their way around her legs and waist. The thorns dug deep into her flesh, blood trickling from every inch of exposed skin. The harder she fought, the tighter the razorweed wrapped her up until she was gasping in pain. She watched helplessly as Timmy slipped farther and farther from her grasp.

In one last desperate escape attempt, Sally broke her piece of crib in two and stabbed the sharp end into the tentacles trapping her. The tentacles unwound from Sally and retreated. Sally then jabbed at each of the tentacles attacking her son until it released his mangled body.

Sally hurried to drag Timmy into their house. Choking back her tears, she laid him on the living room floor. Almost his entire body had been punctured by thorns. Hardly any flesh had been left on his right leg. His left leg—his left leg was missing from the knee-down. And the blood, so much blood covered him that Sally didn't know how he was still alive.

"Mom?" Timmy hacked a wad of blood onto his shirt.

Sally was at his side in a flash. "Timmy? I'm here, sweetheart."

"Mom...wha-what is the date?"

"I-I don't know, dear."

"But...someone asked you...?"

Sally gently grabbed his hand and held it close to her. "Yes. You too?"

Timmy tried to nod but groaned. "Someone...in a suit..." He stared at the bloody cuts in Sally's dress. "Mom, you're hurt."

"It's fine. I need to take care of you—" She tried to move, but a slight pressure on her hand kept her there.

"Mom, please...don't leave me." Timmy's voice sounded sad and childlike.

"I'll just get the first aid kit—"

"Please, it hurts."

Sally looked into Timmy's eyes. The question was genuine, but Sally didn't want to answer it. She only held his hand in both of hers.

"D-dad..." Timmy croaked.

Sally watched as the light in his eyes—the light that shined more brightly than when he hugged her that morning—faded and finally died. His hand went limp between hers. Something inside Sally cracked, and she had to bite her tongue to hold back her scream. She wished she could feel numb, that she could feel nothing, like she had with Celia for those endless days. But something was different this time, and her mix of emotions was too painful to endure: sadness, guilt, rage—so much rage.

Sally stumbled to the first aid kit under the bathroom sink. She patched herself up as best she could before returning to her son. She pulled Timmy's body close to hers, his head cradled against her chest, and lay in the fetal position with him on the living room floor. Hour after hour passed, and pinkish-red daylight melted into pitch black night illuminated only by the distant lights of The Strip. The clock continued to tick. Sally refused to move. Even as her stomach demanded food and her body longed for sleep, she stayed with the body of her child. The clock struck midnight by the time she let her emotions chase her into a restless sleep.

***

He was gone. How could Timmy be gone? Everything was as it had been the previous morning. Even Celia's nursery looked as pristine as ever. She didn't understand. Her dress had also mended, but her injuries remained. Everything that had been broken was now repaired. Everything but her—and Timmy.

Sally paced the living room, running her hand through her hair. The only sounds were her muttering, the occasional cough, and the constant ticking of the clock. After half an hour, her hunger got the better of her, and Sally was forced to make herself some breakfast: bacon, eggs, buttered toast, and a glass of milk.

Partway through setting the table, Sally realized that she had made a meal for three and was putting out dishes for her entire family. Her muscles clenched. Her entire body shook. Her breaths came in and out rapidly as her grip on her glass of milk grew tighter...and tighter...and tighter—

The glass suddenly stuck in her hand and shattered all over the floor. Milk covered Sally's dress and shoeless feet. The white mixed with red on her palm as the cuts began to bleed. Sally took a deep breath to steady herself as she slowly backed out of the pool of milk and glass. She retrieved a towel from the linen closet and began the tedious task of removing the shards from her hand, tears clouding her eyes.

"Alone," she choked out, holding up a shard to her eyes. "I'm all alone." She pressed the glass to the back of her hand and dug in to produce another cut, watching in morbid fascination as the blood slid down her hand. "They all left me."

Sally placed the shards she removed on the table and wrapped the towel around her bleeding hand. She released a dry laugh.

"Everything heals but me."

Sally froze at a tapping on her kitchen window. Minutes passed with only the clock ticking, and then the knocking returned. Sally rose as the knocking grew louder and more persistent. Then another knocking began at the front window. And again at the door.

Maybe Peter has returned with company? Sally thought. *No, he would just come through the front door.*

The knocking soon turned to pounding—on the windows, on the doors, on the walls. No, *inside* the walls. Sally rushed to the center of the dining room. How did it get inside the walls?

Creeping through a mousehole in the wall, the tentacle of a razorweed crawled across the floor and up Sally's leg. Only when its thorns dug into her did she realize what was happening and scream.

Sally tried to run to the kitchen for a knife, but another razorweed tentacle grabbed her ankle and tripped her. She clawed at the carpet as the tentacles dragged her through the now-open front door. She gave another blood-curdling scream as she resisted their pull across the grass, but no one came to her aid. Mr. Johnson continued to mow his lawn, Mrs. Curtis and her grandson continued their gimp down the sidewalk, and Ms. Smith continued to walk her chihuahua as always. Mr. Higgins and his sons were nowhere to be seen as the razorweed pulled Sally towards its waiting mouth.

As it dragged her near her discarded high heels, Sally managed to grab one and started stabbing at the tentacles with abandon. The razorweed's grip on Sally only tightened, and her trek to its mouth quickened. She continued jabbing blindly as she roared and screamed for help that she knew would never come. She twisted and turned in the tentacles' grasp, futilely trying to escape but only scratching herself with the thorns.

Her feet neared its mouth. She could feel the humidity of its breath and the sharp points of its teeth. Another tentacle enclosed her head, squeezing until blood mixed with her tears.

A shot rang out. A projectile narrowly missed Sally and hit the razorweed in the mouth. With a gargling scream, it pulled back its tentacles and let Sally fall to the ground. Just before she lost consciousness, Sally saw the blurred silhouette of a person in a suit standing above her.

* * *

Sally awoke in a bed. Over her stood a figure in a pinstripe suit and a fedora. For a moment, Sally let herself think that it might be Peter. Then what at first appeared to be a skinny man came into focus, revealing a woman with a slight form. Beneath the fedora, the woman sported blonde hair in a soft bob—

Sally nearly fell out of the bed. A *woman* in a suit? Of everything that had been thrown at her the past couple days, this was by far the most unbelievable.

"Who-who are you?" Sally's voice cracked.

The woman tilted her head and removed her hat. "What is today's date?"

Sally growled in frustration. "If I hear that question one more time... It's January 27, 1951, but—" She stopped and stared at the woman. "Wait. It's you. The one who asked me that forsaken question in the first place!"

The woman nodded and set her fedora on the nightstand, beside a pistol. "Yes, I woke you up. And Peter. And Timmy. The name's Alice."

"Peter's awake? Wait, what do you mean, you woke us up?"

"I pulled you out of the time loop we were in."

Sally leapt to her feet but soon collapsed back on the bed, still too weak to stand. "Time loop...we were in a time loop?" Her voice dropped to almost a whisper by the end of her sentence.

Alice tilted her head, looking at Sally with a mixture of curiosity and pity. "Yes. A time loop. Surely you've noticed a lot of oddities since I first asked you for the date."

The breaking of the glasses ran through Sally's mind, followed by the lifeless stares of everyone she saw on her way home from the market. Her stomach churned as she remembered Timmy, his body safely in her arms as she fell asleep and then gone the moment she woke up.

"You could say that," she replied quietly.

"Well, you know the nuclear testing that they've been performing around here?"

Sally's hand balled into a fist around her blanket. "Of course. They told us we'd be safe living here with those happening, but we all know that we're not. They're why Timmy was deformed, why Celia wa-was born too early." She wiped her eyes on the blanket.

Alice hesitated, taking a small step towards Sally before thinking better of it. "Well, it gets better than that. Those tests stopped time."

Sally arched a brow at the strange woman. "Yes, of course. The nuclear tests have stopped time. I assume that the Martians are coming to invade us next, Ms. Welles?"

Alice smirked. "Believe me or not, it's the truth. Do you have a better reason for why everyone around here walks around, doing the same thing day in and day out?"

"We don't do—"

"You wake up every morning and make your family buttered toast, bacon, eggs, and a glass of milk with a side of cough syrup—nice touch, by the way. Your son then goes to school, and your husband goes back to bed because he works nights at a bar at a hotel and casino on The Strip. You take a walk to the market to buy bread, butter, milk, eggs, and bacon and immediately head home. After you put everything away and check on your husband, you have a peanut butter and jelly sandwich while standing at the counter, your one little indulgence of the day. Then you spend the entire afternoon completing your chores. Once Timmy gets home, you help him with his homework—but you don't let him know just how much you're helping him. You want him to think he's getting it on his own so that he'll have a good dose of confidence when he comes of age. Then your husband goes to work at around eight, and you turn in at about nine. That sound familiar?"

Sally shook violently. "How-how do you know any of this?"

"I watched you for what I'm sure was weeks before I finally woke Peter up."

"I mean any of this. The tests, the time loop—any of it! Who are you? Why are you here? What do you want?"

Alice smirked slightly. "Why am I here? I came here chasing the rumors about Jesse Oswell for my blog. Maybe you've heard of him?

Schizophrenic boy? College-aged? Would've just shown up here one day?" Sally's eyes widened at the mention of schizophrenia, but she otherwise shook her head. "Damn—"

"Language!"

"I was hoping that maybe you'd seen him. Thought maybe he was the key to getting out of here, based on some of the rumors I've heard about him since getting stuck here."

"Do-do you really *want* to find someone with schizophrenia? I mean, other than to put them in an asylum..."

Alice rolled her eyes. "Jesse happens to be special."

"So, that's why you're here? To find this...*special* young man?"

Alice rubbed the back of her neck. "Yes." She shrugged, running her hand over the nightstand.

"Well, that's all fine and good, but it still doesn't answer what you want."

"What do I *want*?" Alice laughed dryly. "To wake up whoever I can in order to get us to a better place."

"What do you mean? Wait...Peter...you said you woke him up." Alice appeared about to say something but immediately closed her mouth. "You know where he is, don't you?"

Alice closed her lips tightly. Sally glared at her until Alice could not stand her stare any longer.

"No."

"No?"

"No, I don't know where he is...for sure."

"But you know where he might be?"

Alice sighed. "I might have an idea."

"Then tell me where that is, please."

"No."

"And why not?"

"For one thing, you're too injured."

Sally touched her head bandage with her bandaged hand. She then reached under the blanket, feeling the wrappings around her legs as well.

"So? I'll heal."

"So, you should wait for him to come back. I'm sure he will. He is your husband, after all." Alice's face scrunched up, as though she had tasted something sour.

"How long has it been?"

Alice hesitated. "A week. Maybe more. Time can get confusing here."

"Well, why would Peter be gone so long if he didn't want me to come after him?"

"I don't know for sure. He said something to me about trying to find a way out."

"A way out? Why? This our home! And why would he leave Timmy and me behind?"

"Maybe he wants you to move on."

This time, Sally made a face. "Move on? What does that mean?"

"Move on. Find someone, or something, else. Be your own person, without him."

"He's my husband! We've been together since...since..." Sally paused as she tried to remember when she and Peter first started dating. "High school! We've been going since high school. I can't remember a time without him—"

"Of course you can't."

"What do you mean by that?"

"It's part of this, all this." Alice gestured all around them. "You can only remember things as they've always been on this one day and a life you haven't really experienced."

Sally's eye twitched. "How do you know?"

"I'm a journalist. I do my research. I've talked to the people who've woken up to try and figure out what's going on here and how I can make it better."

"How, might I ask, is that?"

Alice rubbed her jaw. "I don't know, yet."

"What do you mean, you don't know? You are continuing to wake people up when you don't even have a plan for after you do?"

"Look, I don't need to, but I'm going to be honest with you." With Sally's blank expression, Alice continued, "You and your family are the only ones I've woken up so far who haven't decided to go back to their previous lives and pretend as though nothing even happened. That includes the people in your neighborhood."

"So, you are saying that everyone decided to go back to being—wait, my neighbors aren't stuck in that state now?"

"Most of them aren't, no. Not the ones immediately surrounding you. Why?"

Sally gritted her teeth. "They could have helped me with the razorweed." She tried to hold back her tears but was unsuccessful. "They could have helped Timmy."

Alice shifted from foot to foot, staring at the ground. "Yeah, well, people are horrible."

Sally nodded in agreement. After a long moment of silence, she finally said, "I haven't forgotten about you telling me where Peter might have gone."

Alice sighed and rolled her eyes. "I know. I still don't want to tell you."

"Why?"

"Because he's out in the desert. You nearly died in a sparse suburb. I won't have that on my conscience."

"Well, now that you've told me that it's in the desert, I guess I could just start wandering out there. Maybe I will be lucky and not be killed by another razorweed." Sally bit down on her lower lip, trying not to laugh at her own sarcasm.

Alice groaned. "Are you always like this?"

"I think I have a bit more of a personality now that I'm awake."

"So, it's my fault. Great. You know, you can't get where I'm thinking of without a car and my directions, and I know for a fact that Peter took your family's car." Alice grabbed her fedora and started to pick imaginary lint off it. "But I might have a car that you can use, and I might be willing to come with you."

"Then we'll go now."

"We'll go tomorrow. I need to collect food and other supplies." Alice grabbed her pistol and headed towards the door. "Until then, rest."

***

The next morning by sunrise, Alice and Sally drove out of Las Vegas, the desert stretching out before them. Behind them, the city blinked away into darkness. Inch after inch of the desert followed suit, disappearing into nothingness as the two women continued west. An hour into the drive, Sally looked in the rearview mirror to see only blackness.

"Alice..."

"I know." Alice's usually firm voice shook. She gripped the steering wheel tighter. "We'll be there in a few hours."

***

The sun was high in the sky by the time Alice slowed down the baby blue Bel Air. Sally gaped at a sea of orange-gold blossoms swaying in the warm desert breeze. Alice opened her door and stepped out of the car, and Sally followed, still staring at the flowers. A breeze sent yellow spores of pollen drifting in their direction. Before Sally could take a deep, rejuvenating breath, Alice slammed her hand on the hood of the car and startled her.

"Why did you do that?" Sally snapped.

"These flowers are incredibly dangerous," Alice said as she reached into her pocket. She pulled out two cloth face masks and tossed one to Sally. "It's better to be safe than sorry."

Sally watched Alice put on her mask, then did the same.

"So, this is where Peter is supposed to be?" Alice nodded. "I don't see him anywhere."

"Me neither."

"So, what do we do now?"

"Now, we look for clues to see if he ever was here."

Sally nodded, and the two grabbed canteens full of water before going in different directions across the field. Sally carefully swept her section of the field, but dread quickly sunk in. The flowers went on for miles; they could be searching the field for hours and still not find anything. The desert heat was stifling. Sweat dripped down Sally's face, neck, and back, and her lungs burned in less than a half hour of searching. She drank sparingly from her canteen, afraid of running low too quickly. But she wouldn't stop until she knew whether Peter had been there.

***

The sun was about to start setting when Sally spotted a bluish-gray lump among the orange-gold blur. With a sudden burst of adrenaline, she ran to the area and discovered a fedora. Her heart leapt. She picked up the hat and flipped it over. Inside, she found red stitching that said, *Peter Henderson*. Sally smiled. She had sewn Peter's name into the rim of the fedora herself.

Sally looked around and found Alice not far north of her.

"Alice!" she yelled as loud as she could, waving the hat in the air. "Alice, I found something!"

Alice lifted her head and, upon seeing the hat, rushed over. "You find something?"

"Yes. It's Peter's fedora."

"Are you sure it's his?"

"It has his name in it. I checked."

"And you found it here?"

"Yes."

Alice looked at the ground around them. She walked in circles around Sally, bent over as though searching for something. She continued for a few minutes, making wider and wider circles, before returning to Sally's side.

"Odd."

Sally's heart raced. "What?"

"Well, there weren't any tire tracks over by our car, and there aren't any here, either. If Peter had been here, I would think that evidence of his car would have shown up somewhere, especially coming where we came from."

"Well, everything seems to fix itself, so maybe that's what happened to the tracks," Sally argued. "Besides, I doubt that he drove into the flowers."

"I suppose."

"What I don't understand is why he left his fedora behind." Sally turned the hat in her hands, resisting the urge to sniff it for his smell. "He was a proper gentleman. He would never leave his hat behind."

Alice rolled her eyes. "Yeah, I'm sure he was. Well, it's about to get dark. I say we get back to the car and hunker down for the night. Then we can decide what we're going to do."

Sally hesitated before following Alice. "What do you mean, decide what we're going to do?"

"I mean whether we're going to continue with our search or go back—"

"Go back? Go back to what? Didn't you see what happened once we left? Can we even go back?"

"We won't know until we try."

"But what if we try and get sucked into whatever that thing is?"

"So, you're worried about that but not about the other monsters around here?"

"I'm used to those monsters. That...I don't know what that was."

Alice sighed. "Look, we're facing the unknown either way."

"At least we would be doing something productive if we continued looking for Peter."

"You don't know that."

"What do you mean?"

"We don't know what happened to him here. We don't know if he left, if he got transported somewhere like I did—"

Sally's head drooped. "So, you think there's no hope?"

"I'm not saying that. It's just...I don't know. Let's talk about it in the morning."

**

A cross between a growl and a snort woke Sally. Her instinct was to lower herself further into the backseat of the Bel Air, retreating from the complete darkness that surrounded her, but she couldn't. She froze in fear as another growl/snort echoed through the night. She tried to still her breathing and curled up as small as she could. Scraping on the ground made her jump, but she remained as tightly balled up as possible.

"Sally?" Alice whispered from the front seat. The fear in her voice only increased Sally's own.

"Yes?"

"What...what is that?"

Before Sally could reply, something the size of a horse ran up on the car and slammed into the side opposite their heads. The women bit back their screams. The creature rammed into the car again, skidding several feet.

"A nightfright," Sally finally choked out.

The creature slammed into the car again, and Sally prayed that it would not be able to topple the automobile over. Suddenly, the air was knocked out of her when another nightfright rammed the back of the car and sent her rolling onto the floor.

"Sally? Sally, are you OK?"

Alice risked a peek at the backseat, but instead of Sally, she saw the nightfright behind the car. Barely an outline in the night, its dark, leathery, muscular exterior was scarcely visible, but its glowing red eyes towered over Alice and pierced her to her soul. Her mouth grew dry, and her voice disappeared. Her heart raced beneath her ribs. She could not tear her eyes away. Then the first nightfright smashed in the window beside her and dug its teeth into her shoulder, causing her to scream in agony.

Sally regained her composure in time to see the nightfright tearing at Alice's shoulder. Her mind flashed back to Mr. Higgins and Timmy and the razorweed. Tears streamed down her cheeks. Her hand balled into a fist. No. She would not let this happen again.

Sally quickly felt around the floor of the car until she found the flashlight that Alice had packed. She reached over the passenger's side seat and turned on the flashlight, directing it straight at the nightfright's face. With a roar, the nightfright released Alice and retreated into the darkness as Sally followed it with the light of her torch. Still pointing the flashlight at the nightfright, Sally reached back to the ignition and turned on the car and its headlights.

"Alice? Alice, are you OK?" Sally asked as she pulled herself into the driver's seat.

Alice grumbled incoherently.

Sally reached over to the glove compartment, where Alice had insisted on putting the first aid kit. "You're going to be fine. Just stay awake."

Everything that Sally needed to patch up Alice was in the kit. Balancing the flashlight while doing so, however, proved difficult, especially with taking every few minutes to shine it out at the nightfrights when they tried to approach the car. After the bleeding stopped and the shock started to wear off, Alice started to come around.

"How...how did you know to do that?" she asked, nodding her head toward the flashlight.

"Oh, they can't stand the light," Sally replied as she put away the first aid supplies.

"I get that, but how did you know?"

Sally shrugged. "I don't know. I just...know."

"Really? You don't remember learning it?"

"I am certain that I learned it, but I don't remember."

Alice furrowed her brow. "Well, I wish I had known it before now." She sighed. "Maybe I would have one more friend with me."

"I thought you didn't know what these things were."

"I didn't, but that doesn't mean that they hadn't attacked me before."

"Oh." Sally flashed the light at the rear window as the nightfright got too close. "When did that happen?"

"When I first came here. My photographer came with me. We were attacked by these...things the first night we were here as we tried to find civilization. I barely escaped while they..." Alice sniffled. "Well, I escaped." She looked down at the suit she was wearing. "These were his clothes. He always told me I'd get myself in trouble one day wearing men's clothes."

The image of Timmy dying on her living room floor flashed before Sally's eyes. "I'm very sorry."

"I guess it's better that he didn't have to go through this Hell too."

"I'd rather go through H-E-L-L with someone than alone," Sally replied quietly.

Alice glanced at Sally. "You really miss Peter, huh?"

Sally shrugged. "He's all I've ever known. I don't know how I'm going to go on without him."

"For what it's worth, I don't think you'd do badly without him."

Sally smiled slightly. "Thank you. I just wish that he hadn't left without Timmy and me in the first place."

Alice frowned. "Yeah, that was a horrid thing to do, leaving you alone in that state."

"He meant well."

"I guess so."

Sally stared off into the darkness, watching the nightfrights pace while her mind churned.

***

By the time the sun began to rise, the nightfrights had disappeared. Alice had fallen asleep sometime in the night. Sally had turned off the flashlight and the car, but she could not fall asleep herself. She turned Peter's fedora in her hands, examining it as she thought over the memories of their years together. She hoped to find some sort of joy or longing in them, or perhaps a sadness that came with missing him, but she only felt emptiness and disassociation. It was as though they weren't really her memories, the same as Celia's death had been—only this time, her heart wasn't fighting back at the wrongness of it.

Anger bubbled inside her as she thought more about how he left her and Timmy on their own, but she kept finding a way to justify it: he didn't know what was going on, he didn't want to endanger them, he didn't want them to suffer the horrors of being awake like he was until he had everything figured out... None of them could put out the flames of her ire, and thinking on it only made her anger worse.

Sally stared at the sleeping Alice, then at Peter's fedora. She bit her bottom lip before shaking Alice's uninjured shoulder.

"Wha-what?" Alice asked groggily. "Sally? What is it?"

"I have made my decision."

"Decision? About what?"

"About Peter. About everything."

Alice sat up in her seat and stretched with a yawn. "That's a lot to declare first thing in the morning."

"I am serious."

"All right, all right. Out with it."

"Well, I don't want to spend my limited time left looking for a man who left our child and me the first instant that he could." Sally's voice hitched. "Obviously, whatever he saw in me while we were...stuck in time...he didn't see in me...while moving forward. I have nothing left in Las Vegas." She snort-laughed and looked through the rearview window. "I don't even know if it still exists. I want to see what else is out there."

Alice smiled a broad, unflinching smile. "Yeah! That's the ticket! Let's go now. Let's just drive and keep on driving until we run out of gas. Then we'll walk until we can't walk anymore."

Sally grinned, Alice's energy infectious. "All right, then."

Sally rolled down the driver's side window. As she started the car, she flung Peter's fedora outside the window, letting it catch on the breeze and drift onto the ground. The Bel Air raced toward the westward horizon. Behind them, the desert and the fedora blinked out of existence.

The Regular Crowd

Shivangi Narain

There was a stranger at the bar of the Mustang hotel the night Paul's life fell apart. He was hunched into himself on a barstool closest to the window, his brown hair covering his eyes like he was trying his best to go unnoticed. He wasn't succeeding. Canvas shoes and denims, a soft oversized sweater with a hood – he was a sharp contrast to the down-on-their-luck businessmen in sharp suits who usually sat at the poker table. Paul eyed him from the other end of the bar, where he was meticulously wiping down the glasses. Something about him felt... off. The kid barely looked old enough to drink, but though that might have been a problem at the Sands or the Pioneer, the Mustang had a long tradition of looking the other way. No, there was something else that didn't sit right with him. Maybe it was the restless bouncing of his leg, or the tapping of his fingers against the wooden bar counter. Maybe it was the unsettling weight of a curious stare that always disappeared the moment Paul turned to look.

The rag looped the rim of the last highball glass once more as he tried to find something more to do. Old Denny was in his usual corner, nursing his third whiskey. The Roberts brothers had taken their beers into a shady booth and hadn't asked for refills yet. The boys at the poker table had just been topped up. A quick scan of the room confirmed his suspicions, there was nothing left to do but make his approach. He placed the glass back in its rack, upside down but perfectly in line with the rest of the set, and moved over to the stranger. Up close, Paul's unease faded. It was a kid for sure, in college at best. Intelligent, curious eyes found his and widened just a bit, as though he wasn't expecting to be approached. The crimson glow of the sky outside the window only seemed to wash him out, bringing dark shadows under his eyes into painful relief. Paul stifled a snort & plastered on his best bartender smile.

"What can I get ya, kid?"

The boy blinked at him, and Paul willed down a wave of exhaustion. He hated the skittish ones.

"Look, either order something or scram. I got a business to run and-"

"This seat's for paying customers only?" The kid finished, quirking an eyebrow as he took the words right out of Paul's mouth. Quite literally – right down to the tone. A chill went down his spine, but the kid didn't seem to notice. He was too busy giving the hotel a deliberate once over, taking in the quiet mumbles of lukewarm games, sullen regulars, and Edie on stage crooning to a sparse audience of half-drunk gamblers.

"I'll have a cola, I guess, since you're so busy." He said dryly.

Paul clenched his jaw, so tightly he could swear he felt a tooth crack. "Coming right up." he grit out.

The Mustang Hotel wasn't the largest or most successful casino in Vegas, making just enough to stay open from evening to midnight. But it was his, damn it, and he was proud of it. A little out of the way, as close to the edge of the city as safety allowed, where endless red skies met golden-brown sand right outside the window. A hidden gem at the end of the world. When they were testing out in the desert, his customers had the perfect view of the mushroom clouds – one the tour guides at The Sands would kill for. No smart-mouthed kid was going to look down on that.

He schooled his face into something more neutral and handed the boy his drink, in half a mind to charge him double. He watched as the kid sipped at it contentedly, finishing it with an obnoxious slurp.

"Anything else?"

The kid paused to think for a second. "Yeah, actually, can you tell me what day it is?"

"Excuse me?"

"What day is it?"

"What, is that supposed to be some kind of joke?"

The kid looked almost disappointed. "Never mind." He dropped some money on the counter, and slunk out the door.

Old Denny snorted from his corner, "That's what you get, talkin' to these beatnik kids." Paul hummed an acknowledgement, reaching to pick up the money. 12 cents. Exactly double the price of a cola. He had never given the kid his bill. He'd never given him his name, either.

What day is it? The question rung in his head like a gong, echoing as he closed up the casino. He knew what day it was, of course, why wouldn't he? It had been a long one, for sure. He was tired. Tomorrow would be a fresh start.

And so life went on, for a while. Despite the tension building between his shoulder blades throughout the night, the stranger didn't make another appearance. After a week of paranoid glances at the door, Denny eyed him over his whiskey. "What's got you so rattled?"

Paul cleared his head with a shake. "Nothing, don't worry about it." He shot another quick glance at the door. "Guess the kid didn't like his cola."

Denny frowned at him. "What kid?"

"Ah, c'mon Denny, I know it takes more than three drinks to get you juiced. The kid that was in here last week."

Denny narrowed his eyes. "Paul, there was no kid in here last week."

"Quit screwin' with me, of course there was. Sat right over there. I charged him 12 cents for a cola."

"Paul, It's just been us coming in for a while now. Me, Hank and Jerry, and the poker crowd." Denny gave him a once over, "You sure you're okay?"

The question that had been niggling in the back of his mind almost made its way to the tip of his tongue, but Denny was already looking at him like he'd flipped his lid. So he just smiled. "Nothing's wrong, don't worry about it. Just over tired, I guess."

Denny didn't seem too convinced, but he didn't push, going back to his drink. Paul turned away with the question echoing in his head once more. What day is it?

He knocked the same spoon off the counter every day. Edie would sing the same set. Paul found himself humming along. The next day, he broke up a fight at the poker tables before it even began.

That night, he dreamed of the endless desert folding over him. Red skies melding into brown sands like an ocher kaleidoscope. And Paul was in the middle, slipping and drowning, stuck in the funnel of an hour glass. He woke up with a gasp, the static buzz of his bedside radio filling his tiny bedroom. "Have a nice day!" announced the host of his favorite show. Paul turned violently turned the knob until there was only white noise.

He spent a day at home throwing things around his apartment. It didn't help.

"Paul, sweetie" Edie glanced at him through her lashes as she swirled her Martini around in its glass, "We're just worried about you."

This unscripted break in her set was just new enough that Paul was at the very least compelled to listen to her. She placed a hand on his wrist, and he tried not to flinch.

"Let's go out tonight, after you close up. Take a walk on the strip."

Paul gently freed himself from her grasp.

"Not tonight, doll, I'm busy."

He turned away before he could catch the flash of disappointment in her eyes. It would have been a perfectly lovely walk. They would have gone for coffee and stopped to look at the lights on the strip. She'd have held his hand all the way, and he'd have given her his jacket when she shivered. She wouldn't remember anything about it the next day.

"Alright. But you'd tell us, wouldn't you? If something was wrong?"

"Of course."

The question slips through his mind like shifting sands.

One day he cuts his finger on a piece of broken glass and watches it heal over a week. Hank Roberts has had a fresh purple bruise on his left cheek for as long as he's known him. The poker players leave with split lips and black eyes near every night, but come back in fresh as daisies.

Paul might be going crazy, but he wasn't stupid. Whatever the kid – and he was dead-sure he hadn't imagined that encounter – had done to him, it wasn't breaking him. It was waking him up. What day is it? When he stopped to really think about it, it dawned on him that he never knew. It simply was. Yesterday, today, and tomorrow have always been a single entity until now. It was something you just knew, like you knew to brace yourself when the army was bomb testing, or to carry bear spray if you were headed towards the edge of the desert. But just knowing that wasn't enough anymore.

He watched himself clean a highball glass for the hundreth time, looping the rag around and around the rim. What day was it? Fuck it. Paul had decided. Today was Tuesday. Tomorrow would be Wednesday, and the day after would be Thursday. It was like a fog had been lifted from his mind. The change was jarring and immediate, two events superimposed on top of each other – what is, and what should have been. He watched as Jerry Roberts knocked over his beer for the 100th time, but a second later sip from a full glass like nothing had happened. Edie sat at his bar even as she sang on his stage. It was maddening and nauseating, and he had to squeeze his eyes shut to ward off a headache. The glass fell from his hands and shattered against the counter.

"Paul?" Edie's voice cut through the darkness, and he slowly opened his eyes. A quick glance at the stage ensured that this was the only Edie, sitting here in front of him, her face a picture of concern. She grabbed his hand, searching it carefully for injury. He grinned at her, and her frown deepened. "What happened?"

"A headache, that's all."

"That's all?"

"That's all, I'm feeling better already."

She looked at him doubtfully, but returned his smile. "Let me help you clean this up."

"I've got it. But could you do me a favor?"

"Anything."

"Can you remind me what day it is?"

Burned Over

Wade Newhouse

No one in that house wants to hurt anyone.

Grant had written that eight months ago. But now Grant was dead, so maybe he had been wrong.

It was at least the kind of thing you tell an anxious parent—but to honestly make them feel better, or just to keep them away? Matthew Campbell had taken it as both, had kept his emotions in check and done the new thing, which was to let your kids be free to be themselves. But when Emily's letters had changed and she began to suggest that her trip through the desert was no longer a diversion "because of Jesse" and that she might stay out there, he had lost his patience. He remembered the joy she had found upon first discovering *The Canterbury Tales* and the way she had flipped through the giant volume in his office trying to sound it out, and he had supposed that somehow the idea of a pilgrimage in the desert with a new group of friends had brought her back to that first budding desire for adventure.

Of sondry folk, by adventure yfall
In felaweshipe, and pilgrimes were they alle

Grant's body turning up on the highway pushed his escalating concern over these hip pilgrims into a panic.

Earlier, before everything had changed, Emily had sounded excited about him coming to visit, but she had given directions that were both precise and vague. *Beautiful things are going to happen to me. Out of town south toward the mountains*, one letter had said. *Look for two dogs. You have to leave your car there.*

He had no interest in gambling or raucous entertainment and was therefore predisposed to hate a place like Las Vegas, and when he picked up the rental car he scolded himself for being judgmental. The guy at the rental counter was exactly what he had expected: cheerful, pointlessly curious.

"You here to do some gaming?" Round-headed, damp with sweat, smiling. He glanced at the name on the paperwork. "... *Professor* Campbell?"

"No." Matthew's unwillingness to banter seemed preprogrammed into the rental car's routine—he continued on as if this were a real conversation.

"There's plenty to do here. Do you need any tips?"

"No."

"Come on back if you change your mind. I'll always be here!"

Even after ten years he expected Carrie to be in a car beside him. She had wanted to come out west, even back then when there was less to visit. If she knew that he had lost their only daughter to the endless desert she would come back and haunt him, so this was another point against the existence of an afterlife. *You have a savior complex in your classroom*, she would have said, *but you can't save your own daughter.*

Matthew followed the main road "out of town south toward the mountains." He did not trust the strange pinkish tint to the sky, which itself seemed to pulse in the heat the way hot asphalt did in the summer. Many of the other cars on the road had open tops; the faces visible in the ones going toward town seemed flushed, excited, lively, ready to sacrifice themselves to some great god of pleasure. The few that passed him on the way out of town were harder to see but they were hunched down, determined. They were driving too fast.

He had expected the desert to be a flat brown table of land before the mountains, and he was surprised by the amount of detail and texture out here, the detritus from the great city as it had grown and shed people and parts of itself along the way. In addition to small gradations in the landscape and the shrubs and stunted trees that went with it he saw pieces of discarded lives: wooden shacks collapsed on their sides, stray articles of clothing, sun-bleached to a common lifeless pale, scraps of lumber and tin, hand-painted signs. *Repent. Ahead. For Sale.*

He found what he was looking for almost in spite of himself, as if the difficulty of the thing had itself been the challenge and he failed the test by discovering it to be simple: two stone grayhounds standing erect on the left side of the road. In someone else's story they might have been lions or bears, but here their thin sleek lines seemed more obedient than noble. Matthew could not think of a house whose style and aura they might have represented, but sure enough there was a thin dusty road opening between them, the dirt of the path demarcated from the desert only by the vague rut of tire tracks and the relative lack of dry shrubbery.

He felt, leaving the highway, as if he might be trespassing somewhere—as if the entire panorama of desert, distant cityscape and looming mountains might represent a closed system of rules and boundaries to be violated. Did someone own this patch of desert or that one? The borders and limits, if he were in fact moving across and among them, was invisible. But up ahead the land seemed to shimmer and stretch, oily on the near horizon as smaller hills and taller, more skeletal trees began to bunch up to announce the growing nearness of higher ground.

Inexplicably, he saw a flimsy wooden ranch house tucked among the sparse patch of barely-growing things. The entire one-storey structure appeared to lean slightly to the left; it seemed hammered together out of cast-off boards and pieces of lumber never designed for such a purpose. Matthew wondered at how he might describe it back east, and for some reason it reminded him of student essays he had graded for which he could find no comment except unstructured.

As he slowed the car and pulled over off the "road" he suddenly remembered the last of Emily's notes after the one about the two dogs: *You have to leave your car there.* Craning his neck to see how far from the highway he had gone, Matthew decided that whatever concern had inspired that injunction had been rendered void by the new reality of Grant's death and her disappearance.

He stepped out of the car, feeling suddenly too old for this kind of thing. Carrie would have told him to hire a private investigator—surely Las Vegas was filled with the most complex sort with the most arcane and cryptic methods, suited to the darkening pink-hued sky that seemed to press more dry heat down on him from above. He stood there, purposeless. The house seemed not the kind a person just approached, the boards resembling a door too flimsy to be knocked upon. He heard a noise from the brush off to his left, and he drew sharply away from it.

But then he did not need to knock, for the door suddenly flung itself open and a teenaged girl (for a moment, but no—not Emily) slipped out of it and, like a wisp in ratty blue jeans and a filmy blouse, flitted out toward him.

"Come on inside, man! Let's go!"

Matthew had a speech prepared. "Excuse me: I'm Matthew Campbell and I—"

"Get in here, man!" She had grabbed his wrist with paper-thin fingers before he could avoid her, and he found that being pulled along by her surprising strength was easier than standing his ground. There was a rattle of wood and some knocking and pushing and pulling and someone else's hands as the pink afternoon of the outside became a dusty smoke-scented jumble of shadows, whispers, and footsteps. The door shut rattily behind him.

The dim room in which he found himself was more solid than the outside of the house had appeared. There was a coffee table in the middle, standing firmly on all four legs, surrounded by a semicircle of couches. Bookshelves, crammed full with volumes paperback and hardcover, neatly arranged and stuffed excitedly, hovered in the corners. In the gloom there were decorations of some kind on the back wall: a banner, some objects or posters. If there were windows they were boarded up, and the light came from several candles on the coffee table and a sad little table lamp on one of the bookshelves.

But mostly there were people here. Some on the couches, sitting up attentively as if listening to a lecture, others curled up against them like a matinee date. More stood in little clumps around the room, undistinguishable from one another except as vague shapes that were tall or thin or short or wide. The faces Matthew could see were young, probably all under 30, and showed a wide range of skin colors. The girl who had pulled him in was very pale, and she had never let go of his wrist while she had used her other hand to push the door closed.

Matthew started to speak, but the girl suddenly clamped her hand over his mouth, movie-style. He expected her to say "shhh" or to put her finger to her lips, but instead she pressed against him forcefully and stared into his eyes, shaking her head slowly. She was in her young 20s, and the closeness of her eyes made Matthew realize with a start that he had never been this close to a young person since the last time he had seen Emily, over a year ago. His own students were like mannequins to him, posed at desks and lecture tables a wide gulf away.

He was about to pull her hand away from his mouth when he heard something outside.

The sudden mystery of it rose up in his imagination with the strange setting in which he now found himself, and as he listened he felt the sound become a shape. Something swept both past and around the small wooden building, and he felt the shrubs and deadwood trees outside make way for it. Something in the ground thumped and shook, and little puffs of dust rose from the floor while and then changed direction in the air as if gravity itself had pushed and then pulled against itself. A faint whooshing noise abruptly turned into a high-pitched squall and then the whole experience of sound and vibration seemed to gather itself against one corner of the outside wall. The girl's eyes stayed on his, pushing back against any impulse he might have had to move, and then abruptly the outside sound pulled away from the house and everything within hovered in suspended tension for a moment before suddenly falling back into empty normalcy.

The girl pulled her hand away from his mouth then suddenly smiled at him like an excited kid at a birthday party. "You did good, dad. Real good."

Matthew blinked at the word "dad," which he had not heard in so long. He looked past her to the circle of wary faces, wondering if he had survived one danger just to be left in the literal hands of another.

No one in that house wants to hurt anyone.

No one seemed as agitated by the experience they had just experienced as Matthew was.

"What was that?" he finally asked.

"It was Him," said the blonde girl who had pulled him in. Matthew started to ask another question, but the young people scattered around the room began to rattle off their own responses, one after the other, random voices but expected by one another, overlapping, liturgical:

"He is today."

"He is tomorrow."
"He comes for us."

"We go for him."

The words hung in the air between them, and then as if something had been completed the young people began to break out of their small groups and attend to little tasks. Matthew saw now that there were signs of living here: sleeping bags, duffels, satchels, small tables, and that of course there were doors to other rooms. The young people moved with purpose to systematically organize bags, gather books from shelves, pull unseen objects from cabinets, move chairs. The ones who had been on the couches now stood up from them and began to work together to rearrange them into some other position.

The blonde girl took his hand again. "Come on—you're here in time to help."

Matthew let himself be guided through a side door and into a battered, splintery kitchen where another girl, gaunt-thin, was organizing canned food onto little groups. Then he pulled himself free.

"I'm looking for my daughter. Emily Campbell. She wrote me a letter, and I followed the directions she gave me to get here. She's missing."

The girl opened a cabinet and began to pull down some paper plates, separating them from one another and laying them on the counter.

"I'm not Emily Campbell. I'm Carol."

"I know you're not Emily. I'm looking for her. Do you know her? Was she here? Did you see her?"

"People come and go all the time, dad. The ones who are worthy get to stay. He takes the others most of the time."

An image rose to Matthew's mind, an incomplete flash of understanding what might have happened outside if the girl had not pulled him in when the sound had shaken the house.

"What are you all doing out here? Where are your parents?"

The girl named Carol stopped separating paper plates and looked directly at him with something that might have been derision or sympathy. "Cathartes," she said reverently.

The thin girl organizing the cans echoed her. "Cathartes."

"What does that mean? Do you know Emily? Did you see her here?"

Ignoring the new tone rising in his voice, the girl named Carol said again, "You are in time to help."

She took the plates back into the main room, and the other girl followed her with as many of the cans as she could carry.

The room had already been transformed: chairs and couches were now in an approximation of a clumsy half-circle, two rows deep, like seating for a small orchestra pulled at random from a junkyard. The crooked, cheap-looking coffee table in the center had two half-melted candles placed upon it with a battered paperback book between them.

Matthew tried to pull Carol away from her task, which was now handing out one paper plate to each of the other kids who were completing their own jobs of moving and arranging and were now standing upright in stations around the room. When Carol attempted to give him a paper plate as well Matthew knocked the rest of the stack from her hands and turned out to the room and the twenty or so placid faces that watched him.

"Look, I'm sorry I interrupted you. I'm not here to help, and I'm not here to get in the way. I'm just looking for my daughter. Her name is Emily. I think she might have come out here a few months ago. She gave me directions to get here. I can't find her and I'm looking for any information that you ... information that anyone might have about where she might have gone."

There was a low rustling murmur as the young people appeared to whisper opinions to one another—the subject of their speech was indistinct. Carol raised her arms and gestured for order.

"This man was very lucky to get here when he did. He might have chosen him. Maybe he is here for a reason, and we should help him. Does anyone know someone named Emily who might have visited us?"

The group again consulted, shared words in low murmurs. Someone standing in a shadow suggested, in a stuttery voice, "Check the casinos in the city. People never leave there!" This was met by a tittering of shy laughter that rippled around the room. Matthew felt the nervous hysteria that had simmered in him all day beginning to tilt into rage. The low laughter rippled from person to person, becoming little conversations and gesticulations, and Matthew impotently sought some way to break through it. He raised his foot up high and then brought it down violently upon the wobbly coffee table, which collapsed under the assault and spilled its candles and book into the dirt.

"Tell me something, goddammit! I know you know something! Tell me!"

From the back wall, a plaintive voice: "Maybe she has gone to be with Cathartes."

Then, silence, itself more maddening than the strange community that refused to tell him what he wanted to know. Whatever had animated them was gone now, and for the first time he felt fear creeping in the spaces between them. More sudden and dour than when the house had shaken from the impact of the thing sweeping by outside, this was a thin thread of anxiety that Matthew felt twisting through the room, uncontrolled. These were no longer self-confident brats playing at some kind of sleepover camp but children, like Emily herself had seemed to him when she first started her journey no matter her legal age. In their eyes was a collective need to be taken care of and comforted. He thought randomly of the guy who rented him the car—the only adult he had spoken to today. *I'll always be here!*

"What is Cathartes?"

Someone in the back—maybe the girl who had spoken the word—held up a candle toward the back wall, and for the first time Matthew saw that it was not a decoration hung on the wall but a sprawled-out object—

A bird—a large bird—with its wings extended three or four feet across like a giant black angel and its face, red and shriveled, twisted off to the side, yellow beak hooked and agape in dead rage. A ... vulture? Buzzard. (*What is the difference?*)

The girl who called herself Carol stooped down and picked up the book that had fallen from the coffee table under Matthew's foot. Birds of North America. The entire volume was dusty, battered, torn from a cycle of overuse and neglect. Its spine was broken open to a particular page, where a photograph of an open-winged vulture topped several paragraphs of facts, lists, a habitat map.

Cathartes Aura.

Matthew pushed the book away. "Who the hell are you kids? What are you doing out here?"

Carol pointed to one of the other young people—a white kid, all skin and bones with a scrawny attempt at a beard—and gestured for him to come forward. "Go see what He has taken. Bring this dad with you."

The thin kid stepped forward obediently, pushed past Matthew, and started to open the door. Matthew moved to intercept him and put his hand against the wood.

"What about the thing outside? Whatever you pulled me away from?"

The other kid stared at him blankly. "He comes for us. We go for him."

Carol gently pulled Matthew's hand away from the door. "But His time is past now. You can go out." Then, as if she had meant to say it but had forgotten: "By Cathartes."

"By Cathartes." A general, badly-rehearsed murmur from around the room.

The thin kind went ahead with his task of opening the door, so Matthew ducked in behind him before the door closed back behind him.

It was getting darker, or at least later. The sky that had had a pale rosy tint to it earlier in the day had now assumed a thicker tone, almost like a pink bruise, and it pulsed. Something polluted it. There was a heavier electricity in the air, too: it felt to Matthew that he could snap his fingers and create sparks between his fingertips, or maybe run a battery by running his hands through his hair.

The kid did not wait for him but headed off down a path scratched in the brush, off to the left and then around to the back of the house.

"What's your name, son?"

"Sam."

"It's good to meet you, Sam. I'm Matthew. Can you tell me about what you kids are doing out here? Where are your parents?"

"We go to Him."

"And He comes for you. Yeah, I heard that. But why? Why out here?"

But Sam had stopped abruptly, and Matthew looked up to see what had prompted him, and his mind went blank with shock.

Someone had been here, but whoever it had been was no longer recognizable except as a shredded mass of bloody clothing and gory fragments that might have been pieces of a human body but were now just strewn about in a red and black tangle of crushed undergrowth that glistened wetly in the light of approaching evening.

"Good Christ," whispered Matthew. "What is this?"

"He comes for us. We go to him."

Something in the flattened circle of blood and destroyed tissue might have been a shoe, and Matthew felt himself becoming light-headed and nauseous, and then he saw on the edge of the remains a length of bloodied rope tied to a small, stout-looking shrub.

"Oh my god," he said. More terrifying to him than the implication of the bloody remains and the rope was the blank emptiness in Sam's face. *He has seen this before. He has seen this over and over.*

"Sam," said Matthew quietly. "You kids need to get out of here. Back to town."

Something might have been stirring in the shrubbery, or sounds might have been echoing down from the higher ground looming on the near horizon, or he might have heard merely the frantic hot panic that was rising in his own mind. Without waiting to ask whether Sam heard them as well, Matthew grabbed the boy by his bony arm and pulled him violently back toward the house's increasingly fragile-seeming door.

The others were waiting there, eyes wide and bodies tense. Before Matthew could start to scream out the exhortation he had not even yet conceived, Sam managed to cry out "He comes for us," and there was a rising wail of acknowledgement, jubilation, and affirmation from the rest of the group, which then in a swarming dirty mass threw themselves at the back wall and bent, in various kneeling and half-standing protestations, before the dead vulture spread out and nailed there. The cries and murmurings grew louder, the bodies rocking and jerking became more agitated and frenzied, and Matthew stood apart from them, the horror at his alienation from this ritual spiraling out from the nausea he felt at the image of the mutilated corpse (sacrifice) that still colored his sight.

The crying became wailing, and interspersed with the inarticulate rising and falling voices he heard over and over again the word "Cathartes" jabbered and chanted, and he felt a great sweaty heat begin to swell up from the group, a ferocious energy that he felt himself being pulled into despite himself. As he watched the group of young people become a congregation and then a mob he remembered that he had spent his life standing before such groups: giving them reading assignments, leading discussions, urging contemplation. He heard *Cathartes Cathartes* and watched delirious spittle fly from cracked lips and filthy hair shake with ecstasy and remembered suddenly the lessons he had taught about revivalism in the nineteenth century, a spectacle he had ticked off rationally from a series of notes without once taking time to imagine what it must have sounded and smelled like. Charles Finney had documented it:

I found that region of country what, in the western phrase, would be called,

a "burnt district." There had been, a few years previously, a wild excitement

passing through that region, which they called a revival of religion, but which turned out to be spurious

Had Charles Finney seen the terror and fury and prayers for salvation, smelled the blood of sacrifice and the filthy sweat of the people in the burned over district as one spiritual craze and then another swept through tiny communities connected to one another only by the wild-eyed sermons of traveling preachers? Had one warned of the rage of the monster that could be appeased only by leaving a sacrifice tied to a desert tree? Surely the next one testified that only prayers to *Cathartes Aura* would save them. Charles Finney and Matthew Campbell had seen them only from a distance.

Without a thought, as if the hysteria of the room had reached him but translated its energy into something unique for him, Matthew grabbed the kid nearest him and threw him violently into the mass of mourning worshippers, which now collapsed like a scattered mass of bowling pins. The cries of *cathartes* melted together and died out in a great exhalation of shock and exhaustion, and Matthew hurled himself at the great dead bird on the wall as if he might tear it down with is own clawed hands.

"Listen to me! Stop and listen to me, goddammit!"

Sudden silence and slack-jawed impossible stares.

"I don't know what you are all doing here, but you need to get out of here. Something out there is dangerous and this—*this*—isn't real. You all need to grow up and get your shit together and *get out of here.*"

A plaintive voice, pleading, from the crowd: "He comes for us. And Cathartes—"

"*Cathartes isn't real!* Jesus Christ..."

Stillness. Dirt hung in the air like conversation.

The girl who called herself Carol appeared out of the crowd, impossibly calm but with the lines of tears streaked down her dust-mottled face. "Cathartes protected you when He came. Cathartes protects us all."

Then, one part of Matthew's instinct gave way to another, and he felt again that rightness he had felt in the classroom in all those lessons before when a student had protested or complained and he had simply surrendered to their need to tell. He gathered himself together and stood as tall as he could make himself. The adult in the room. Dad.

"Show me," he said.

The girl who called herself Carol might have smiled, the way a little child does when a parent agrees to watch the dance they have spent an hour preparing. She held out her hand and Matthew took it, stepping over several young people who had flattened themselves on the ground before the vulture altar.

Thanne longen folk to goon on pilgrimages

He had not seen the door on this side of the room, opposite the one he had taken into the kitchen with the cans and paper plates. Carol took him toward it now, and Matthew was hit suddenly by the smell coming from the other side: mossy, stale; rotten leaves and sulphur and neglect. Her hand on the doorknob, Carol turned back to him and her mouth was a smile without emotion. "Cathartes."

Behind them, a low weary murmur from the group. "Cathartes..."

The room was tiny and dark, something that must have once been a bedroom because the only object was a collapsing, misshapen bed, a distorted shape in the dark where tiny lines of pink light came in between boards nailed over long-broken-out windows. The smell came up in thin hot waves that Matthew could almost see, and something was tied to the remains of the bed.

A girl, thin and splayed out like an insect on a pinboard, except not an insect. A bird.

Matthew saw what was left of Emily's lime green polo shirt, one she had proudly showed off to him in a photograph sent from California on the first leg of the trip that had led her to Las Vegas. Both it and her favorite tan shorts were almost unrecognizable—not because of the humid gloom but because her entire body was covered with—*feathers?*

Matthew imagined a chaotic kindergarten class in which a roomful of children had been given a human model tied to a bed, a sack of long black and gray feathers picked up from half-eaten corpses in the desert, and a bucket of blood for glue and then told to make a bird—a vulture ("Let's say it together, children: *cathartes aura*"). What would the results look like? Feathers plastered on in every direction, some by the gory handful, clotted together with blood and strands of rotted flesh, some weakly stabbed into whatever part of the body would hold them: belt loops, button holes, behind the ears, between shaking fingers.

Here eyes, just visible between the flaccid mass of blood and feathers, rolled back, twitching. Her hands were tied loosely to the splintered, broken posts of the bed, and they too twitched, flexed, twisted. There was a small clumsy table beside the bed, and on the table were several paper plates smeared with what Matthew assumed was more blood but then he realized was in fact half-eaten pasta and sauce from the can sitting beside it.

The presence of the food and her twitching limbs told him that she was alive, and he was throwing himself to her almost before the door was completely open. He heard Carol behind him, speaking about "Cathartes" and "salvation" and "protection," but he was already pulling away the thin ropes from the bedposts, so obviously tied by inexperienced young people (*children*) playing at something they had seen in movies. He was murmuring her name while her eyes fluttered, unseeing, and he pushed away feathers and blood to clear her face, which was bruised and crossed with scratches and small lacerations.

Now Carol became alarmed. "What are you doing, dad?"

"Getting my daughter the fuck out of here." Her arms flopped listlessly from the released knots, and her head rolled into his chest as he lifted her from the bed, pausing to thrash away more of the feathers that clung weakly to her small frame. He heard her murmur "Daddy" and that word fueled him like adrenaline; with her in his arms he turned to the door where other young people had crowded behind Carol to watch this drama.

"No, dad," said Carol warily, and he could see an agitation growing in the wan faces behind her. "Cathartes protects us all."

"Obviously not very well. I saw what was left of someone outside with Sam. Get out of my fucking way."

Now the murmuring ripple of voices whispering *cathartes* was spreading again, and as he gathered his strength for what he knew was coming he again saw behind this mass of scared children the faces of the townspeople in the New York hinterlands awaiting that season's new testament and revival circuit in the first decades of the 1800s. Sin, death, judgment, repentance with no beginning or ending to anchor them to the routine of life. Once locked in, each day the same grasping at a fleeting meaning learned only through jubilation passing through until the next entertaining voice came along. Charles Finney had had an *anxious bench* where sinners were harangued and made to cry for salvation—these dirty desert rats sacrificed themselves under a pink sky and prayed to a homemade carrion-eater for protection from their last end.

Matthew Campbell knew that faith growing from fear could turn quickly into rage and violence, so without giving this dirty congregation time to process what was happening to their bloody ritual he tucked Emily more tightly against his chest and turned his shoulder forward like a football player. Then he charged forward, trusting the momentum of their bodies and his own anger to carry him through the forest of wailing and grasping arms that were now in his face, tearing at his jacket, filling his nostrils with rank, fetid desperation. Bloody feathers dropped from Emily's body as he pushed forward, and some of the faithful grabbed at them, tried to stab them back onto her.

Finally he was back at the little house's front door where Carol had first held him silent to protect him from Him. The terror that must have first created this community spread out from there, and the young people were unwilling to get too close to it. With the young people torn between wanting to stop him and hesitating near the door, Matthew gently set Emily on the ground before it and wrenched it open.

The lateness of the day had settled the pink sky into an easy approximation of a typical desert sunset, and his rental car was still there where he had left it. But now it was ... decorated? Adorned with something that Matthew had to squeeze his eyes shut for a moment to process.

Vultures—actual, living birds—now crowded in the twenty yards between the door and the car. Presumably drawn here by the body in the woods, as the first ones must have when these kids had taken refuge in the house however long ago, they wandered awkwardly among themselves, their beaks red with what they had found. Some of them fluttered indignantly and hop-flapped back in the direction of the scene Sam had shown him in the brush.

Then this ebony bird beguiling my sad fancy into smiling

He heard another sound in the near distance, somewhere beyond the immediate screen of brush and small trees, and he felt again a strange tremor in the ground and air. "Oh Jesus ..."

His own fear was validated by a seeming wall of hysterical terror rising from the people in the house: a horror growing from real and lived experience with this thing that came out of the desert and killed them horribly one by one. Matthew ran to the car, shoving the ungainly fowl from his path, and opened the passenger side door, then ran back to the house and scooped Emily up in his arms even as Sam appeared and struggled to close it with her body blocking the way.

As he fumbled to put the key into the ignition the vultures themselves took note of whatever was coming for them.

He comes for us

and began to take flight, knocking against one another with their huge wingspans. One of the bloody feathers that had been plastered to Emily now stuck to his hand, and he brushed it away in disgust. As he peeled the car randomly backwards in a circle, crushing shrubs and tiny branches underneath, he saw in a blurry half-vision some black shape lurching quickly out from behind the house and a dozen thin dirty arms struggling to push the door shut. Then his foot was on the gas pedal, back down the road to the highway, and the noise behind him might have been the shattering of wood beneath the jaws of something he had not seen or it might have been the slamming of the door and the impotent rage of a hunger denied again by luck and timing.

He heard his daughter making sounds beside him, her eyes still half-closed and stinking of carrion, and he remembered the smiling words of the car rental salesman: "I'll always be here!" He felt, as one danger receded behind him in a haze of screaming—perhaps of agony or perhaps of jubilation—that there must be many tiny congregations out here on the frontier of the city that was always expanding, always reaching out for more land to swallow and souls to steal. Charles Finney, leading the fires in the burned-over district, had called his own conversion an *impression, a wave of electricity*, and Matthew Campbell wondered at the kinetic thrum he could still feel in the air, and he grieved for the children who had lost their angel.

Downwinders

Henry Snider

James Reynolds gripped the steering wheel of their 1990 Taurus station wagon tighter. Heather was asleep, red hair masking her face as she lay curled against the door. But his wife wasn't the problem.

"God, Rory, you are such a little snot-weasel." An audible smack followed the insult.

"Bitch!"

"Rory!" Heather sat up straight, their seven-year-old's insult snapping her from an hour-long nap.

"Well, Marin called me a snot-weasel and hit me!"

Heather turned in her seat. "Marin—"

"Rory," James cut her off before yet another mother-daughter fight could get off the ground, "what, exactly, did you do back there to be called a snot weasel?"

"Marin was texting her boyfriend about how much she loves kissing him."

James's grip went from tight to white-knuckled. He caught sight of Heather taking a deep breath before she responded in a calmer tone. "Rory, you've got your own phone, and a game system. Focus on one of those rather than what your sister's doing."

"But she hit me."

"You heard Mom," Marin said. "Mind your business."

The inevitable whine reared its ugly head as their son droned out, "Buuuuuuut—"

"Rory," James snapped and looked at his son through the rear-view mirror long enough to make eye-contact with the boy. "Enough." The word sounded flat, but carried the threat of what would happen if this conversation continued.

Dejected, Rory slumped and looked out the window.

A slight pull to the left put the car centered in their lane again, giving James another opportunity to chance a look at his daughter. Hair, the same shade of dark red as her mother's, was pulled back in a tight braid, giving him a perfect view of the smirk worn as she returned her attention to her phone.

"James...." Heather's single word said, "Speak to your daughter, too. Balance this before it gets out of hand."

"Marin...."

The car thrummed as it drifted onto the center line and ran over the road's rumble strips.

"On the road, Dear."

He grumbled a response while easing the car back into their lane. "Marin?"

"M-yeah?" She didn't bother looking up.

Heather was still turned around and watching. "Marin Elizabeth Reynolds."

The phone went down out of sight of the rear-view mirror. "God! Yes?"

James mimicked his daughter's smirk. "Don't get caught next time."

"James!"

"Yes, Daddy."

Rory screwed up his face and snarkily mimicked, "Yes, Daddy."

James turned the mirror up so it only reflected the car's ceiling.

Heather situated herself facing forward again. "That wasn't quite what I wanted you to say."

"Eh. He was goading her. A smack on the arm is a hell of a lot better than what she could do once we're out of the car."

She reached down in front of the seat and came up with a bag of chips. "True. Nothing worse than being teased when you're thirteen."

Jesus. Thirteen. It didn't matter that Marin was thirteen and a week. No matter how he looked at it she...was...thirteen. He could feel her pulling away a little month by month, trading the innocence of childhood and doting parents for friends and now boys.

"Kissing," he mumbled.

"Mmmmm hmmm," Heather confirmed, crunching on a mouthful of chips.

"Fuck me," he said, even quieter.

"That's what got us here in the first place."

Her comment hung in the air for a moment before they both burst out laughing.

Rory asked, "What's so funny?"

"You," James said.

"Your sister," Heather added.

"Your mom."

Heather grinned, showing chip encrusted teeth and nodded ahead of them. "How long before you get around these guys?"

They'd been ascending the pass for the last fifteen minutes, but were stuck at the end of a convoy that occupied both westbound lanes of the Colorado highway for over a half hour.

"I don't know how. There's at least...what, twenty of them?"

The two rear vehicles drove in parallel, silhouettes of soldiers occasionally shifted, but overall, the view remained the same.

"C'mon, Dad," Rory chided, "pass 'em."

The steep grade leveled out as they came around a bend. And overlook, complete with bathrooms was cut from the mountain pass.

"Dad!" Marin exclaimed.

"Yeah. Bathroom." He braked and turned into the empty parking lot. The car barely came to a stop before both rear doors opened and their kids shot out and darted towards the restrooms.

Crisp air blew, reminding James why they kept jackets within easy reach.

Afternoon light left long shadows reaching from the lone building.

They got out, mimicking each other with a stretch.

"Should we worry?" he asked.

"About what? An ice-cold toilet seat?"

Fifteen minutes later they were all standing in front of the overlook posing for a family picture when the air pressure dipped.

"Woah," Rory said. "Did y'all feel that?"

Heather turned toward the direction they'd just come. "A storm, maybe?"

A boom came, rumbling up the valley in front of them. Birds broke from the trees in every direction before coalescing into a single mass heading south.

Then another boom sounded.

And another.

James snapped, "Get in the car."

No one moved.

"Now!"

As one, all four Reynolds ran to the car, got in, slammed doors, and buckled up. James started the wagon up and tore back onto the road with tires sliding on the sandy shoulder.

"James," Heather said, instinctively putting a hand on the dashboard, "you're scaring me."

He eased his foot off the gas as they rounded the first curve and began their descent on the far side. For the second time in under a minute the tires slid, starting a fishtail. He released the wheel and let the car straighten itself out.

"James!"

"I know this sound, this...feeling. Those are gas tanks exploding." He eased the car back up over fifty on a straightaway. "We heard three—"

"Four," Marin added. "One when we were running."

With eyes focused on the road ahead of them, he continued. "Those idiots were packed too tight. I knew it."

Heather shrieked as they came around the next bend. "Slow!"

"That car lot that went up when I was a kid? Same God-damned sound."

Rory asked, "They wrecked?"

"I-I think so."

"Damn it, James! If you don't slow down, we're going to wreck, too!"

He took his foot off the accelerator and let the car coast to a more manageable speed, but couldn't help keeping his foot hovering over that pedal rather than moving it to the brake.

Trees whipped by, nothing more than green and gray blurs against red rock. Sunlight still shone down, cutting beams through the trees.

Another bend.

Another curve.

"There!" James took a hand from the wheel and pointed to one of the few breaks in the trees. Charcoal smoke snaked up, thick and oily, marking where the wreck was.

Heather reached out, left hand going from the dashboard to his thigh. "What are we supposed to do?"

"I don't know." Another turn left him going all the way into the other lane before getting the car under control. "Whatever we can. Marin, do you have any signal?"

"Dad...I...yes! I've got three bars!"

"Nine one one. Let them know where we are and what happened."

"But we don—"

Heather cut in, with a calmer — but still tense — tone. "When we get there, baby. Just tell them what we know and what we see. Answer any questions."

They skidded around a narrow corner and saw a Hummer off the road and about ten feet up a tree, burning. The driver hung out the door with a face so covered in blood telling gender — much less anything else — was impossible.

The next straightaway opened up, showing the caravan scattered everywhere. The semi they'd surrounded lay on its side; trailer split open like tin foil with a fist punched through it.

Orange and gold fluttered everywhere from the trees, across the road, snowing down over the entire wreck site.

James slammed on the brakes, jerking the wheel to the left to avoid hitting another Hummer resting on its side just as a soldier darted from behind the vehicle waving his arms to make them stop.

The Taurus skidded forward, momentum refusing to be denied as its front impacted the soldier, folding him at the waist before he slid up and onto the hood.

Screams came from inside the car, matching those of the injured lining the road.

Orange and gold snow continued to fall.

Petals...those are flower—

The ground dropped out below the car and daylight swirled to night as the scene, trees, even the other vehicles were swallowed in an obsidian pit tinged in those obnoxious petal colors. Air, somehow heavier than what they normally breathed, resisted being pulled into lungs. A last glimmer of light gave the impression of their car rocketing away from the accident, images growing smaller until only a pinprick remained.

James barely had time to register that they were falling before the car struck solid ground again.

Bang!

Are they shooting at us?

A bloody handprint marred the windshield.

"Are we...," Heather started, the remainder of the sentence forgotten as she stared at the immobile soldier on the hood of their car. Only the portion of the man pressed against the glass was visible, the rest masked by darkness.

James turned in his seat and looked back at his children. Marin sat wide-eyed, taking in the same thing Heather was, while Rory's head darted back and forth, staring out at the darkness around them.

Heather finally spoke again. "We're in a sinkhole. We've got to get the kids out!" Her seatbelt unbuckled and she opened the door to hard-packed sand beneath her feet. "I...." The glow from the car's interior reached for around ten feet, showing nothing but dry, hardpacked earth."

The driver's door swung open and James stepped out, flicking on the lights as he did so. Fifty yards of dry, firm sand lay ahead of the vehicle. He looked up. A few stars winked above them, with more discernable as his sudden night blindness subsided.

A groan brought both parents back to the front of the car. A dark streak covered their hood ending under the soldier, whose right had held onto the passenger side wiper.

Rory's door opened.

"Stay in the car," Heather said.

James leaned over. "Hey...buddy, can you hear me?"

Rory called out, "How can it be night?"

"Nnnyeauuuugh," escaped the soldier on a shuddering breath.

Heather leaned into the car. "Marin, back on the phone, now! Nine one one, just like Dad said."

Marin didn't move other than to blink, gaze firmly fixed on the windshield. Tears brimmed but hadn't fallen.

"Marin!"

James looked past the man and into the car, seeing his daughter jolt as if stuck with a pin.

"Ma...Ma-Mom. Yeah," the teen blinked hard and looked down to unlock her phone.

"It...hurrrrrrts," came from behind James, making him turn around and bump the soldier's leg, eliciting a groan from the man.

"Who's out there?"

Only quiet and darkness.

James squinted, not being able to make out anything. "Heather, get the flashlight." He didn't dare turn away.

Another groan came from the hood-bound soldier as he felt the car shift. A beam cut a dusty ray over his shoulder lighting up the silhouette of another Hummer, this one still on all four wheels. The passenger door hung open, showing an empty interior.

"Down here."

The light slid from one fender to the other, angling down to the truck's front. Under the front end lay another soldier, looking maybe twenty at the oldest, judging by his babyface contorted in pain. The front passenger side tire rested squarely on the man's right forearm.

"Little...help?"

James ran to him, accidentally kicking dust under the vehicle and right into the man's face as he came to a stop. "Shit. Sorry."

"Least of my—"

A gust of wind picked up, pelting them with dust. James ran around to the driver's side and opened the door. "Sorry," he called down as he climbed up into the military vehicle and froze. Where the hell did the key go? Where the hell was the slot for the key in the first place?

"James," Heather called from the car.

He ignored her and continued searching for either the key or at least a key slot. A moment later he heard strained laughter.

"Left side, top."

"What?"

"The starter."

James got out and down on one knee. The soldier was nothing more than shadow haloed by Heather's flashlight.

"The starter," he repeated. "The top left of the dashboard. Turn the switch to run, wait for the light to go off, then turn it to start and let go."

He got back in the vehicle and followed the instructions. An amber light came on, and after about ten seconds, winked out. A single turn on the switch fired the vehicle up. James reached for the transmission and froze. Forward or back? The wrong choice could rip flesh from the man's arm.

Indecision was the only answer. He pushed the brake, put the Hummer in neutral and eased up on the pedal, letting gravity make the decision for him. It rolled forward a foot and he stopped, killing the engine and jumped out.

The soldier was still on the ground, though now cradling his arm and lying on his side, still lit by the flashlight's beam. A growl of pain came through gritted teeth.

"Easy, now. You're okay."

"Fuck! It was better when the tire was still on it."

James made out dim features...typical military haircut, dark hair, those same baby-faced features he noted before. Essentially, what he figured everyone expected when hearing the word "soldier."

The light disappeared as Heather went to the back of the wagon, opened it, and dumped the contents of the food box into the junk box sitting beside it.

"Heather—"

"In a minute." She came trotting over with the flashlight bobbing, trapped in her armpit as she carried the box and what looked like a handful of snakes.

The doors on the wagon, save that of the driver's door slammed one by one as Marin climbed around in the vehicle, the last being the hatch her mother left open.

Heather dropped the box and, what ended up being a clutch of bungee cords by the soldier. James knelt along with his wife as she took to tearing the corners of the box sides, leaving a flat plus sign of cardboard.

"Is it broke?" she asked.

"The fuck do you think? A truck dropped on me."

"Hey," James said reflexively.

"S-sorry."

"It's okay," Heather said. "I need to see it...."

"Gilley," he finished. "Mason Gilley." Mason rolled slowly onto his back, leaving the injured arm resting on the ground. Heather gently felt the upper arm, getting only a slight groan from him. The same when she cupped the elbow.

"You a medic?" Mason managed.

"Seven brothers," she said, pulling the flashlight free from her armpit and shoving it at James. "Point it here." The beam was directed at Mason's forearm.

"Seven, huh?"

"Three older, four younger." She reached across to Mason's good arm and used a bungee to measure from wrist to elbow. "All stupid," she added and compared the length to the injured right arm.

"Got four, myself," he said, voice sounding calmer. "All girls."

"That sucks," James said.

"Good. They're the same length." She looked up at James. "It means there's no compound fracture...or at least no obvious one."

"We're here," Mason said, looking up into the night sky. "I can't believe we're really here."

"Where?" James felt the reality of what was going on nipping at his sanity.

"I'm going to lock this in for you, Mason...going to make a cast of sorts."

"You are a medic."

Heather didn't even crack a smile. "Like I said, stupid brothers. I've made one or two of these before."

Through enough vulgarities to make a sailor cringe, they got Mason into a sitting position so the make-shift cast could be fitted to him, she made a cardboard tube out of the short wall of the box, wrapping it around his upper arm and securing it with a bungee cord, leaving the corner linking it to the box's bottom. It was gingerly placed around the broken forearm and secured with another two bungee cords. The fourth she hooked from the top of the cardboard on the upper arm down to the end of the tube by his wrist. The final two cords were linked together and looped over his head, making a sling.

"There," Heather said, eyeing Mason. "What do you think?"

"I-I think I'm going to throw up."

James stood and stepped back while his wife stayed where she was, supporting the injured arm slightly.

"Mom...," Marin called from inside the car.

"We're fine, honey," James answered for her. "We'll be back in just a minute."

Something roared in the darkness, its shriek something more like an engine coming apart due to lack of oil.

Something close.

"Car," Mason said, suddenly more coherent.

James and Heather started helping him up. He shook them off before vertigo gripped him again. He staggered, but repeated, "Get in the car! Now!"

James gripped Mason by the belt and started dragging him around the front of the car. When his wife moved to help him, he snapped, "No! Get behind the wheel." He dragged the soldier to the front passenger door and pulled it open, unceremoniously shoving the injured man into the car, slamming his door, then pulling the rear door open in time to see Rory dart over the back seat and onto the luggage. Getting in, he wished he'd taken the time to move the front seat forward. His own door was slammed for him by something impacting it with enough force to rock the entire car.

"I don't believe this," Mason said. "I'm here and I still don't fucking believe this."

"What the hell are you talking about," James asked, leaning close to the headrest of Mason's seat.

"Seven-sixties. Locals call them 'Night Frights.'" He shifted in the seat and gave an unmasculine squeak. "The dome light...turn it on!"

Rory said, "No, Dad! It'll see us!"

Mason's voice softened again, sounding muddy. "Seven-sixties are afraid...ofthelight, "he finished quickly, sucking in air at the end from a new wave of pain.

Whatever was outside pressed against the car again, rocking it.

Heather flicked on the dome light, making everyone wince at the sudden brightness. The Taurus shifted back to its original position.

"Mason," James said, doing his best to not sound overly threatening, "what is out there?" He took a second calming breath, reminding himself the other man was injured, in shock, and in the same boatload of crap as the rest of them. "And where are we? It's the middle of the afternoon and it's suddenly midnight. There must be—"

"A...L...T...Zero...Three."

A growl came from outside the rear hatch and Rory climbed back over the rear seat, cuddling into James's lap and draping his legs onto his sister. Both gripped onto him.

Heather held the flashlight, now off, as if it were a weapon. "What is that? Some kind of call sign?"

Mason's head hung, but he answered. "Yes...no. I—"

"Where...are...we?" James punctuated the last word with a finger jab to the back of the soldier's head.

"It's a...." Another sigh, this one full of resignation. "It's the designation of an alternate reality."

"Bullshit," James blurted.

"Let him finish," Heather said and gave him a warning look.

"It sounds like bullshit," Mason confirmed. "But it's not. ALT Zero One is so hot we cooked three techs before they could shut it off. Microwaved the hell outta them."

Marin said, "You mean—"

"Radiation," Heather finished.

Mason offered a weak chuckle. "Give the lady a prize."

"Christ," James muttered, "Are we—"

Mason cut him off. "We're fine." He craned his head in an effort to see James. "I mean, we're fucked, but we're fine."

"There's no growth anywhere around," Marin said. "How do you know we're not there?"

"In Zero One?"

"Yeah."

A handful of seconds ticked by before he responded with, "If this were Zero One we'd already be dead. Besides there were Bloom Flowers."

The flowers all over the road. They brought us here?

Mason answered the question as if James had actually voiced it. "They seem to be in every reality." He chuckled. "Ever wonder how so many people could go missing over the years and are never found?"

Reality settled in, putting an uncomfortable ache in the pit of James's stomach.

Rory shifted. "Ow, Marin, you're hurting me."

James looked over at his daughter. Pure terror filled her eyes as she stared at the windshield where the other soldier lay.

"He blinked," she screamed. "He blinked!"

Everyone's attention went to the glass.

The man, mid-forties, face leathery and blood soaked, stared into the car. His one visible eye slowly moved from Heather to Mason.

"I didn't even see him," Mason said. "Lieutenant Briggs."

Heather reached for the door handle. "We should—"

Mason's left hand darted out, snagging her right. "If you open that door we're dead. We're all dead. There's a...there's something out there. And it will grab you, drag you off, and eat you...all while the rest of us sit here and listen." He let her go and pointed out the driver's side window. The hummer's silhouette was clearly distinguishable, with a lightening purple glow outlining a mountain ranger in the distance. "If we just wait a little longer, just a little, the sun will be up."

James scoffed. "So, we all get to die in the daylight?"

"No. They can't be out in the daylight."

The Lieutenant moved, shifted his head, letting his face slide down the windshield six inches. His split lip gapped further, showing the bottom row of teeth, sans two which were broken off.

Heather looked from Mason to her husband. "James, we have to—"

A low growl came from the driver's side of the car, echoing through the vehicle more like the idling of a muscle car.

Heather started to shake, nearly dropping the flashlight onto the floorboard. "It's...afraid...of...the...light?"

Mason nodded, staring past her and into the darkness outside.

She turned, raised the flashlight and flicked it on. Light reflected off the glass, blinding her and everyone else in the car. A figure, not as dark as the pitch around it, jerked back from the car, but not before a glimpse of the ebony predator was washed in light. Split nostrils flared on a snout short for its body, but huge, nonetheless.

It was the eyes that transfixed James. They glowed a neon green when hit with the light. A single snarl and it was gone.

James asked, "Can we get him now?"

Mason shook his head. "Once they smell blood...." He let the rest of the sentence hang.

"Puh-Puh," came from Lieutenant Briggs, spittle mixed with blood fell from the split lip's "V." "Please."

His voice didn't match the man's size, coming out nasally, almost high pitched.

James looked at the back of Mason's head as the soldier looked down. He reached forward and grasped Heather's elbow, getting her attention.

A chuff sounded in front of the car.

"Turn the headlights on, Mom," Marin said. "Turn them on...please turn them on. Mom...Mom...Mommmm!"

James let go of his wife and grabbed both his children, pulling them to him and burying their faces into his chest. But he couldn't look away. All three adults stared into Briggs's widening eyes as he was pulled off the hood.

Heather gripped the steering wheel similarly to James had when all this started just a few short minutes ago.

Christ. Had it only been a few minutes?

The screaming started as soon as he slid off the hood. It was weak, wet, and pitiful.

Heather dropped the flashlight from her left hand and reached for the headlight switch.

"Don't," Mason said, cradling his arm for the first time since they'd dove into the car. "He's already dead. Briggs just doesn't realize it yet. It's better this way."

They sat in silence, listening to screams fall to crying whimpers, until the only sound coming from outside was tearing as meat ripped from bone.

Half an hour later the sunrise lit the sky with radiant yellows, oranges, and reds. Overhead, the sky was still a deep purple, fading into black behind the Taurus.

James wasn't sure if the kids had fallen asleep or were well on their way to catatonia. Either way, the crying had stopped not long after the sounds of feeding ended.

"Mason," James said, voice not more than a whisper.

"Yeah?"

"These things...is it safe to get out now?"

"Fuck if I know." He groaned and adjusted the bungee cord slung around his neck. "We got a pamphlet and an hour lecture on this place. That's it."

Heather's lip quivered. James watched it unsure of whether this meant she was upset or about to unleash hell on the man seated next to her.

"What is happening?" She looked at Mason, leaning in, fury apparent. "Where are we? What is going on?" A breath puffed out, steaming the glass. The action not all that different from the one the predator expelled against her window. "You tell me now, or by God a broken arm is going to be the least of your worries.

"Easy now," Mason said.

Heather reached out and gave him a shove, bringing a wince and hiss of pain. "Think I'm playing?"

"Ow! All right! All right!" Mason shifted in an effort to put more room between them. "Might as well wake the kiddos up. If we're all going to get through this, it's gotta be all hands on deck."

Marin's muffled voice said, "I'm awake." She sat up, still holding onto Rory's feet. Her makeup showed no signs of tears and barely any smudging.

James shook his head, wondering why in the hell he'd notice something so trivial. "Rory."

His son shifted, burying his face into James's shirt.

"Rory," he repeated.

"Mmmm-yeah? Are we there yet?" He sat up, sleepy face turning to dread as reality set in. "Not here. I don't wanna be here."

He gripped the boy's shoulders, meeting his gaze. "We don't want to be, either. Mason's going to tell us what's going on so—"

"We can go home," Rory finished.

Mason asked, "Is there anything to drink?"

Marin rummaged over the back and passed a bottle of water up.

"Thanks." The bottle was gone in three long swallows. "Where the hell to start?"

Heather kept looking out the windows, taking in the desert landscape around them. "Try the Cliff Notes version. We can ask questions as you go."

Ever the teacher.

"We found ways to alternate realities."

Rory sat up, pulling his legs down and in-between James and Marin's. "You mean other worlds?"

"Same world. Different reality."

"What's the difference?"

James looked out his window, The sun was getting close to cresting the ridge.

"I dunno, kid. Like I said, I just got transferred a week ago, and got the class and the ticket here today."

James spoke over Rory, who was about to fire, what he assumed to be, a barrage of questions. "Can we get home?"

"Probably. Depends on where the blooms dropped us."

Heather adjusted her braid, which was well on its way to coming undone. "So, you're saying we could be anywhere."

"Are you guys familiar with the Nevada Testing Site?"

James leaned his forehead against the window, feeling the cool glass against his forehead. "We were going through Nevada on—"

"Wait," Heather cut in, "We're in Nevada?"

"We're in a Nevada, yes."

"Heather, Rory, let him finish."

Mason didn't start back up right away, leaving everyone waiting, and started to shift. "Looks bright enough to get out now." He moved to reach across with his good arm to open the door. James reached over the seat and placed his hand on the soldier's shoulder, gently pulling him back against the seat.

"We'll get out in a couple of minutes...when the sun's a little higher. In the meantime, finish."

"The blooms always drop us in the testing ground somewhere. With the concentration we were hauling we're guaranteed to be in Yucca Flat somewhere."

Heather started, "But—"

"Hey, like your husband said, shut it so I can finish."

She did.

"The more blooms, the closer to the highest concentration of radiation we land."

"Did you say radiation," Heather asked.

"What did I—"

She gripped the flashlight like a baton. "Radiation?"

"We've been inside the car for most of this, but yeah."

James thumped his head against the glass. "How bad?"

"Depends on the wind, but bad enough we're going to get a good scrubbing and swabbed...if we're lucky."

"And," Marin added, "if we're not?"

Mason yawned. "Do I look worried? They've got decontaminants. It just sucks."

James released the shoulder. "You're saying we're in the other Nevada on a testing range. We're being exposed to radiation and there's mutants running around?"

"You sound like me a few days ago."

Heather looked out the windshield, adjusting herself to see around the bloody dried smear Briggs left. "How do we get home?"

Mason took the opportunity reach over and open the door. No one moved to stop him. He stood, bracing himself against the car so he didn't drop. "Whoa...wasn't expecting that."

The other three doors opened, and everyone stepped out, Rory climbing out behind James.

The sun broke over the peaks, bringing an orange morning into full light, sharp shadows dragging long around them.

Rory stayed pressed against James, asking, "What about the...."

"Those night fuckers?"

"Hey," Heather said, "Nice."

Mason smirked, looking down at the boy. "Sorry." He enunciated the word in that oh-so-typical up yours sort of way. "The locals call them Night Frights. I've heard 'black death, desert chickens,'" A chuckle came, making him wince. "Hell, even 'preachers.'"

It was Marin's turn to scoff. "Preachers?"

"You see 'em and the next thing you know you're closer to God than you planned on being."

Heather walked to the front of the Taurus, looked down and purged her stomach's meager contents.

"I'll keep talking, but we need to see what the situation here is."

Rory repeated, "But the—"

"Night Frights," Mason finished. "They can't come out in the daylight. We're golden as long as we stay in the light."

Heather finished and stood, wiping her mouth with the back of her hand. "Kids, back in the car."

For a rare change, neither argued and got back into the rear seat, closing the doors behind them.

Heather moved to the rear of the car, avoiding whatever remains were left at the front. "We'll help. The kids stay in the car."

Mason opened his mouth to comment, and James just made a slight shake of his head, letting the soldier know it was a battle he wasn't going to win. A pained smile cracked the dried dust coating his face. "Fair enough. The first thing is to see if we can reach anyone."

The three went around to the Hummer, with Heather retracing her steps around the back of their wagon. Morbid curiosity overtook the men, and they looked down as they passed the bloody mess. Briggs's lower body was missing, leaving him on his back, one arm still up, and gripping the bumper in death. The corpse had been hollowed out, meat missing on the inside of his ribcage all the way down to the bone. The jaw was missing, leaving the head as a graphic caricature of someone screaming. A wet spot under the headlight punctuated where Heather vomited.

It took Mason two tries to climb into the Hummer's passenger seat. He looked at the dash, muttering to himself. "You left the engine on."

"I...sorry."

"Good thing we don't have that far to go." He rummaged in a bag he found on the floorboard, pulling out a map and notebook filled with notes. Grabbing the mic, he clicked it several times, and waited.

Only static came from the speaker.

James looked in, careful not to bump Mason's arm. "Shouldn't you speak into that?"

Mason made a pfffft sound. "Reception's for shit here anyway, but no," he wiggled his knee supporting the notebook. "I'm not supposed to do anything other than key a few times. If they respond we follow protocol."

A morning wind picked up, pelting them with dust. James winced, thinking of radioactive particles peppering against his skin. He looked at Heather, seeing the same thoughts running through her mind.

"Come on." Mason keyed the microphone again.

Heather stepped back, looking across the flat terrain. "Are we too far away?"

"No. It just doesn't always work the way it's supposed to. Radio...people...animals...." He stared out the windshield. "Hell, even the physics doesn't always work like it's supposed to."

Heather kept looking into the distance. "What are those divots?"

James followed her gaze, seeing pock marks marring the desert floor. "They're—"

Mason cut in. "They're detonation sites."

James looked at the sheer number of them, way beyond what he thought the nation had tested over the decades.

Mason played with the radio a bit more but got no response. "Well," he said, "guess we're driving.

Heather looked from the open door back to their car. "I don't think our car's going anywhere. We've got a flat and the drop...."

Mason leaned back in the seat. "We'll take this."

James turned and started back to the wagon. "We'll be ready to go in just a few minutes. Just have to get a few things."

"Leave it," Mason said. "They'll burn it all, anyway. It's all irradiated."

"And us?" Heather asked, "What about us?"

Mason's grin masked the grimace of pain. "Like a glow stick. I've already said they've got treatments. We'll be fine."

James grabbed the food box, cooler, and jackets for everyone and loaded them into the car before taking a seat behind the wheel. Mason sat beside him, leaving Heather and the kids occupying the back seat. Rory fought with Marin for the window seat, ultimately losing and resigning himself to the middle.

James put the Hummer in drive. "So, where to?"

Mason motioned with his head to the south. "Get down onto the flat, then try not to drive down in any craters. It's bad enough we'll be skirting them."

Rory asked, "Why?"

Mason just cut a look at James before splitting his attention between the road and cradling his arm against the constant jostling of the military vehicle.

It took nearly a half hour to come off the rise and down onto the desert floor. Eroded grooves deep enough to swallow a tire made the going slow, but James finally managed to navigate them.

James looked south. "Just avoid going through the craters?" Dimples seemed to mar every inch of their path. "Not sure that's possible."

Mason shifted, pulling his arm tight against his ribs. "Just do the best you can. Map said we should hit a road sooner or later."

They drove at a snail's pace for the next hour, barely topping five miles per hour. The first crater they skirted was deep, its center down a good thirty feet. At the deepest point vegetation bloomed in the shadows. Hues of green, purple, and yellow carpeted the ground.

Marin cleared her throat. "What kind of plants are those?"

Mason didn't look. "The kind you don't mess with." He fumbled with the bag of paperwork before settling back again. "Gonna close my eyes. Just keep going in this direction. Turn when you get to the road."

They skimmed two more craters, one pitted off the edge of another. The only way past them was to go down into the larger pit, riding the rim bordering the smaller, second one.

"James?"

He adjusted the rear-view mirror to see his wife. "It's fine."

They descended down into the crater, its shadow swallowing them. The instant they dipped below the rim the air felt hotter, rousing Mason.

"What the actual—"

"There was no way around, so I—"

"Floor it!"

James didn't ask why, he just stomped on the gas, and jolted the vehicle forward, spitting dust behind them.

The ground vibrated, seeming to hum so violently that everything became more of a blur. The truck slowed, still spraying radioactive soil into the air.

Twenty miles per hour....

Fifteen....

Ten.

James glanced at the side mirror. Gray weeds, freed from the layer of dust covering them, tangled into the tires.

The vibrations intensified, making his bones hurt.

Their Hummer pulled free, lurching forward and climbing up and out of the depression. An immediate jerk to the left kept them from descending into a neighboring crater, which had its floor already blanketed with the same growth they'd pulled free of. The same vibrations shaking dust from this plant as well.

"Dad," Marin said, "it's moving." Her voice sounded detached, not really in the moment anymore.

Hell, James thought, what would be?

"Dad," she repeated. "Dad...Dad? Dad!"

Mason looked out the passenger window and yelled, "Faster!"

James leaned forward and out the same window. The plant wasn't just vibrating, but actively shaking dust from itself. And it wasn't just big, it was huge. Dozens of sage green leaves unfurled and dug into the earth, pulling the core of the plant free. Each bladed leaf cutting into the crater floor as an oar through water, propelling the plant forward.

The truck started to dip to the left, back into the crater they'd just pulled out of. Another jerk of the wheel had them fishtailing between the two detonation sites. James took his foot off the gas and let the Hummer slow.

Mason turned his head away from the passenger window. "Stay...out...of...the...craters. They're not just hot—"

"No shit," Heather said, voice sounding rough.

The truck continued to slow as they cleared the ridge between the craters and hit a patch of flat ground. James asked, "Can we get out and pull any vines from the axle here?"

Mason shook his head. "Go up a ways. I want a little more distance between us and...that."

They continued south for another ten minutes before James repeated the question because the truck felt sluggish.

"Fine," Mason agreed. "Just do it here, and everyone," he got louder, "and I mean fuckin' everyone, keep your eyes open. Each of you pick a direction and watch. Holler if you see anything...a dust devil, a prairie dog...whatever. You see anything, you shout. Got it?"

All four of them murmured in agreement. Mason added, to James, "When you step out, step wide in case it's worked its way up the undercarriage."

James did as asked and, after opening the door, actually jumped free of the vehicle, landing a good six feet away. He landed wrong and stumbled a few steps before standing upright. He looked back at the car, hunting for any movement in the shadows.

"Looks okay," he called.

"Then come around and let me out. I can't get it open with my arm."

As he walked around the front, James took the opportunity to take in the valley. So many craters pock-marked their path he didn't know how they'd manage to get from here to the road without going through dozens of them. "There are so many," he said. The sky kept shifting. An even orange haze went from ridge to ridge, yet every so often patches of blue sky, once with the hit of a white cloud in the distance, would appear. Not as if wind made a break to see through, but just come into existence for a handful of heartbeats before fading away again.

"Like a mirage," Mason called out. "Move it." James quickened his pace, came around and opened the door for the soldier. He climbed free, nodding to the machete resting in a door-mounted sheath. "Better bring it."

James grabbed the blade and noticed the difference between this and the one they'd bought a while back at a camping store. The machete felt heavier, and springy compared to the stiff one they'd bought.

"Listen," Mason said as they rounded the back of the Hummer, "We took some real heat back there."

"Radiation?"

Mason nodded. "We clean this up, roll up the windows, and get moving. Stay out of the craters no matter what."

James's stomach sank. "Are we going to...?"

Mason smiled. "Detox is going to suck for all of us, but we should be okay."

James knelt and started inspecting the rear bumper. "Shots and the scrubbing you mentioned?"

Mason pointed to the where the bumper met frame on the driver's side where a finger-wide length of growth hovered, its tip tasting the air much like a snake would.

"It's...." James struggled for the right words. "It's alive."

Mason snorted a reply.

The length of vine...bush...hell, Little Shop of Horrors come alive probed at the bottom of the vehicle. James poked at it with the end of the machete. The plant's response was immediate, wrapping around the end of the blade and nearly wrenching it free from his grip.

"Son of a bitch," James muttered and jerked back hard, bringing a good three-foot length of plant with the blade.

"Strike the edge against the earth. Cut it free!"

He did as told and swung against the ground, edge cutting through dusty green vegetation each time it was buried into the soil. A half dozen strikes later James stood, weapon freed, and looked at the small scattering of plan life. Each piece still moved, though now lazily, similar to earthworms he'd segmented in some biology class from high school.

The rear passenger window rolled down and Heather called out, "Do you think there's any more down there?"

James opened his mouth to reply, but realized he didn't actually have an answer. He looked over to Mason.

"Maybe. Best we get a move on it. Even if there's more underneath, there won't be enough to gum up the wheel."

They climbed back in, James taking the time to help Mason. Both men took an additional second to stare at the bottom edge of the Hummer before getting back in.

Once back in motion, James sped up, moving them at nearly thirty miles per hour. Knuckles white, he kept them as close to the crest as possible. Each crater had at least one growth carpeting the bottom, hues of sage green, purple, and yellow jutting through the sand innocently probing the air and offering no hint as to the predator lurking just below the surface.

"Didn't expect to say this, but you're going a bit too fast. At this speed, if you cut the wheel wrong just once we'll bog down and be stuck walking. Believe me, we don't want to—"

Soil gave way on the right side, tipping them into the largest crater yet. The sudden dip jolted the unseatbelted Mason up fast enough to hit his head on the roof before slamming back down into the seat and slamming forward, face-first, into the dashboard.

James muttered, "Shit, shit, shit, shitshitshit," while turning the wheel and pointing the Hummer down into the crater. The walls of this one were steeper, ensuring any direction other than down would result in them rolling. His family screamed while Mason just bounced around his side of the cab, body sliding partially down into the leg well. Blood spattered the dash where he'd impacted.

The temp rose as if opening an oven.

By God, this his huge. This one crater has to be close to a mile across rim-to-rim.

Heather's hand gripped his shoulder from the back seat. "He said not to go driving in these again!"

He gripped the wheel, stepping on the accelerator. "Wasn't my idea!" His gaze darted left and right, taking in the crater wall's steepness. Seeing the lowest point to the left, James kept applying easy pressure to the gas, inching it forward without wanting to lose what limited ability he had handling the Hummer.

The heat increased, making that itch at the back of his neck worsen.

"Daaaaad," Marin screamed. "It's another...." Her sentence didn't finish. Rory's own yelling fell silent.

Jesus. Heather's grip is killing me.

The crater floor shook violently and the right two tires lost grip for an instant, sending a plume of loose dirt up into the air.

Something big was closing in on them, something just at the edge of his vision, moving fast.

He looked to the right, taking in what appeared to be the bastard child of a spider plant and a tumbleweed. Supporting stalks grew thicker than James's thigh.

Heather's warning echoed in his head. Eyes on the road.

What road?

They shot across the crater floor, peaking at nearly seventy. Fireworks danced behind his eyes and he tried to blink them away. They started pulling away from the plant.

Flashes of white kept drawing his attention from where they were going.

"James," Heather said loud enough to hear, but far from the level of screaming done over the last several seconds. "Go faster."

The white flashes happened again. he looked this time.

Bones.

Interwoven Throughout the plant predator, bones shone white against sage green in the morning light. One, a skull, sat haloed by the tattered remnants of a yellow scarf, giving the impression of a nighmarish demented crown.

James eased off the gas a touch.

"No," Heather repeated, "faster."

If the side of the crater's too soft—"

Bam!

Something struck against the side of the Hummer, cracking the passenger side rear window.

"...we'll drive into the side and not up it!"

The front of the vehicle tipped skyward, following the incline of the crater's wall.

Sweat dripped from James's face, his hands...everywhere.

Sixty.

Fifty.

The plant struck the passenger window, spidering the glass. The rearview mirror gave another view of the skull he'd seen seconds earlier pressing into the glass, forcing the opening larger.

He floored it, hoping the forward momentum would get them out of the crater.

Fifty.

They were at least maintaining speed. More soil crumbled under their wheels. Then the truck's front continued skyward as they pushed over the crest, tires slamming down, and jolting everyone around.

James didn't slow. The nightmare vegetation crested only a second behind them. The horizon leveled, then dipped as they started down a smaller crater. The plant in this one shook free of the dust and moved toward them at breakneck speed.

"No," was all James could muster.

The foliage shot past them, leaves streaking dirt from the side of the Hummer as it skirted the vehicle. He jerked the wheel, angling them back up the crater's side. The side mirror allowed a view as the two plants impacted. The sound, loud enough to be heard over the engine reminded James of cheerleader pompoms being shaken. A cloud of dust engulfed the plants, hiding their battle.

He took his foot off the gas as they exited, turning back onto a good stretch of flat land.

"Don't stop," Marin said, head craned around and looking out the rear window.

"He's not," Heather said. "Dad's just putting more distance between us and...them."

A couple of minutes passed before James asked, "Does anyone see anything around?"

No one responded, though everyone, save the unconscious Mason, scanned the area surrounding them.

"Just dirt," Rory said.

The Hummer slowed.

"No, Dad!" Marin's voice verged on shrieking. "Don't stop!"

James pointed out the windshield. Fifty feet ahead of them lay a road crossing their path. Little more than two ruts, it still offered potential salvation.

He stepped on the brake, skidding them to a halt.

Marin leaned forward, only to be kept from climbing into the front seat by Heather's efforts. "Go!"

James snapped, "Which way?" He turned to look at each member of his family in turn. "Left? Right? Continue across it and keep going south?" He motioned to Mason, crumpled in the foot well of the passenger seat. "He knows which way. I don't." He took a moment to pinch the bridge of his nose, clenching his eyes shut. "If I keep going south, we could end up in another crater. We barely made it out of those."

"Then...," Heather hesitated and stared at the road, eyes following it as far into the distance as possible. "Then we follow the road."

He looked at the ruts. "Is this even a road?"

James put the vehicle in park and leaned over, gently feeling Mason's bloody neck.

Rory asked, "Is he alive?"

A laugh, sounding more like a bark, escaped James. "Hell if I know."

Heather's hand reached up, fingers lightly touching his own. "He's alive. He's breathing."

Rory tried to push up alongside Marin, who was still partially wedged between the seats. "We need to help him."

Father and mother shared a look, coming to the same conclusion without saying a word. Heather pulled back on her daughter who, begrudgingly released the headrests and dropped back into her seat.

"We're not doctors," Heather said. "We could hurt him more by moving him."

"And we can't stay here," James added.

"But—"

"We're going to follow the road. All roads go somewhere, and anywhere but here is a good destination."

Heather let go of James's hand, leaning back into her seat. "Left or right?"

Left...east, had the nearest range of mountains - the same ones they'd been skirting since they hit the flats. To the right led out into the flat but posed the best bet for finding people.

James offered, "Right?"

No one answered again, leaving this decision up to him.

Without another word, he turned right, and headed west, keeping the wheels in the ruts of the road.

Twice over the next half hour they had to go overland, skirting craters that erased entire sections of road. The second time Mason convulsed as the vehicle jostled over the rough terrain, blood spewing from his ruined face. James kept his eyes ahead of the vehicle, ignoring the soldier. Behind him, his family did the same, each making the conscious decision not to acknowledge Mason's condition.

"Wait," James said. "Is that...." He pointed out in the distance where something winked brightly in their direction.

"Glass!" Heather yelled in his ear.

Too far away to make out much of anything beyond darker smudges around the reflection. Though not sure exactly what they were looking at, it was definitely something.

Heather dropped her voice to a calm level. "Don't speed, Honey. Just get us there."

As they approached, a handful of buildings seemed to rise from the earth. In the center a radio tower stood as a wire-framed skyscraper.

Marin leaned her head against the doorframe, squinting against the dust blowing in through the broken window. "How much farther?"

"A mile or two. Less than five minutes at this pace."

Mason groaned for the third time in as many minutes.

Heather said, "Sounds like our tour guide is coming around."

James glanced down. Mason hadn't moved since landing in the footwell. There was so much blood...and his face. The two impacts against the dash had mangled his features to little more than a caricature of what they once were. Wounds bore a shiny sheen bordered by coagulated runoff.

The town — if it could really be called that — was a dozen or so structures, with the first few made of concrete. Rectangular openings showed where windows and doorways would go when construction was complete.

James honked the horn, the tone bleating in contrast to the size of the vehicle. Marin leaned closer to the door and moved to put her head out the broken window. Her mother's hand grasped the teen's arm and gently pulled her back.

They crept to the middle of town, stopping at a wide point between houses. A street sign signified the narrow gap was meant to be a crossroads.

He hit the horn again, this time stirring Mason.

A few of the buildings were recognizable. A tiny movie theater, complete with marquee advertising Armageddon, a café with dusty glass making up the entire front of the building, a couple of tract-stye homes, a one-roomed schoolhouse built to mimic larger brick ones, and a church marking the end of the town. James put the truck in park and climbed out. The concrete frames they'd passed on the way in had the same basic fronts as the two completed tract homes. He started walking down the middle of the street.

"James," Heather called. "Stay with us."

He stopped, not turning back to look at her, and stayed focused on the buildings. "There may be a phone, or...something."

He crossed to the left side of the street, looking in the café. Putting hands to the side of his face and pressing it against the glass offered a dim view of tables, chairs, and two people seated across from each other.

"Hey!"

They didn't move. The man, dressed in casual clothing faced a pony-tailed blonde. Two plates of food sat on the table between them.

James ran to the door and ripped it open, racing inside.

The lights were on but flickered and dimmed. A radio hissed static somewhere back in the kitchen. The couple never acknowledged him, remaining immobile.

The door opened a second time and Heather entered, trailed by their kids. The three of them stopped and stayed at the entrance.

"Dad?"

"Rory, you guys stay there, okay?"

"Are they dead?"

James walked over to the table, eyeing them suspiciously. They couldn't have been over thirty. Each sat slumped in their chair, heads tipped forward, and eyes closed.

Marin parroted her brother's question. "Are...they...dead?"

"No," Heather answered for him. "They're breathing."

He stood beside them and studied the couple...trio, he corrected himself as a stroller sat low that he'd missed before.

They were dressed for summer, both wearing identical khaki shorts and t-shirts. James reached out to touch the woman's neck.

"James! Don't!"

He looked over to his wife, nodded, then picked up a napkin from the table and touched the side of her head. It lolled to the side without resistance. The sales tag for the shirt was still attached at its short sleeve. That's when he noticed the scab at the crook of her elbow.

Right where someone would get a shot.

The man had an identical spot on his arm.

James gave a stern look to Heather and moved around the table to the stroller. The blanket lay half-draped over the sleeping child, a tuft of brown hair crowning its head. Tucked in beside him was a nearly empty IV bag.

Grabbing the stroller, James pushed it over to his family. Heather looked quizzically at him, and Marin bent to pick the child up.

"Leave him. Let Mom get the IV out first." He pushed past them and stepped outside. "Wait here. I'll be right back."

Fifty feet later he was at the front of the theater. Behind the ticket booth glass, an acne-scarred teen sat slumped in the same way as the couple in the café. James jerked on the door and stepped inside. The narrow building didn't have a concession area but went from doorway past a curtain and right into the theater proper.

The projector was on, firing bright light against the screen, though nothing actually played. The combination of light and shadow gave a stark shadow-puppet feel to the place. James moved down the aisle, counting out fifteen people occupying the seats, every single one slumped in the same way as the first couple.

Memories of junior high history classes surfaced, choking off his breath.

Mock towns.

Mannequins populating the area.

James's stomach clenched as he felt a thump in his bones more than anywhere else in his body. Everything around him seemed to drop, like an elevator slipping. He fell into the nearest seat, cracking his nose and the armrest. He pushed himself to his feet and staggered up the aisle, an overpowering vertigo pulling him off-center with each step taken.

The door opened into the bright midday light and James saw his family, with Marin now carrying the baby, as they exited the café. Everyone made for the Hummer and Rory pointed past the buildings.

In the distance, a wall of sand raced toward them, flowing like water over the flat. Beyond it, a mushroom cloud folded in on itself as it grew, traveling skyward.

They piled into the truck and James pressed the starter.

Nothing happened.

"Shit!"

He reached over and switched the starter to run. The blast was coming so fast — so...damned fast — then pressed the starter when the light went off.

The Hummer fired up and James slammed the car into drive, skidding between the buildings and stomped the gas pedal to the floor, racing out of town on the same rutted road they'd entered from.

"Block up that window," Heather screamed and the kids turned and rummaged for whatever they could find behind the rear seat. A cushion came around in Rory's hands and he reached past Marin and pressed it against the opening. Marin shifted and leaned a shoulder against it, holding the seat in place.

James looked out the passenger window. The blast was nearly on them. Marring the glass, he focused on the words I SAID SOUTH written in bloody smears.

"The fucking bomb just went off in the south, asshole," he grumbled.

The author still lay in the footwell, though shifted from the position they'd left him in. A single eye was visible, and it focused squarely on James.

Sixty.

The Hummer bounced in and out of the ruts at breakneck speed.

Seventy.

"Oh...shit," Heather said as she looked out the windshield to where they were going.

Suddenly the truck was moving faster, racing toward the rim of a crater as if being fired from a gun. The Hummer rose, rear end rising higher, giving everyone a face-down view of the craters edge racing by twenty feet below them. That distance grew as the crater dipped below them. The lip fell from view as they continued a slow tumble through the air, propelled by the latest nuclear test.

Gravity gripped the vehicle, pulling them down fast. James gripped the wheel and closed his eyes the earth raced up.

***

Everything hurt.

He couldn't get a proper breath. It felt like sucking air through a straw half submerged in cup of water.

"Heh...hehh...."

Someone was speaking.

"Heh...."

James realized it was him. "Hea...ther?"

He could hear sobbing, but it sounded a thousand miles away.

Open...your...eyes.

James forced his eyes open, unable to easily focus on the two steering wheels in front of him. Closing his left eye to the severe double vision seemed to help.

By some miracle they were right side up. Mason was inverted in the passenger seat, his upper body wedged down into the footwell and his right leg bent awkwardly mid-shin.

"Hea-ther?"

His head felt full of cotton, making thinking, much less hearing a near impossibility.

Why is there a baby crying?

More sobbing, but the voice sounded familiar.

The Hummer was struck from the passenger side, skidding it several feet.

He moaned.

Something raced past the front of the truck.

James made out a small blurry form disappearing into the storm.

"No," He whispered as Rory vanished from sight.

"Heather?"

More crying.

Marin.

It was Marin's voice.

Did her boyfriend break up with her?

No. That wasn't right.

He could see movement. Seconds ticked by before James realized it was being reflected by the rear view mirror.

Marin was over the back seat, knees pulled to her chest and rocking a small bundle. Her eyes darted from his, to the broken window. Heather's head and shoulders pressed out the hole, blocking most of the dust from getting in. Her body twitched, then convulsed, thrashed, before slowing, her breath hitching with each inhalation.

"Marin."

The teen's only response was louder sobbing.

The side mirror reflected Heather, face up, head tilted back, struggling to get a breath around a length of plant growth forcing itself down her throat. James saw the vine stab forward a foot. His wife's legs kicked out once...twice...then fell still.

"Mar-in!" Blood spat from his mouth, peppering his side of the windshield. He looked down. The lower half of the steering wheel disappeared into the bottom portion of his ribcage.

"Oh."

The word sounded stupid...sounded moronic even considering the circumstances, but somehow fit the answer to the questions at hand.

...to every question he'd ever had.

It was getting harder to see.

He was so tired.

Heather was pulled free of the Hummer, letting the wind howl in.

She must be going to look for Rory.

He closed his eyes and listened as sobbing turned to screams.

So high pitched...almost musical.

It must be birds.

I hear birds singing.

A Scent of Blood and Flowers

Josh Snider

A gentle patter of rain filled the air with the scent of petrichor, small drops sending ripples across scattered puddles. The rear parking lot sat mostly empty, the owner too cheap to have more than three people on the clock at any time. Half of the lot sat in an ankle-deep pool, sure to sink further after the storm cleared and the water drained away, taking the sand underneath with it.

Cheap bastard.

Trey leaned against the aging brick wall and took another drag from his cigarette. Stocking the convenience store was supposed to be a temporary job, just enough to save over the summer and get out of town. That was three years ago, and here he was, trapped in a dead-end job in a dead-end town with a nearly dead car.

Hot smoke filled his lungs as he took the final pull, the cherry glowing brightly before being dropped onto the wet pavement. The cherry on the end of his cigarette lit up brightly in the dim afternoon as he took the final pull of hot smoke, lungs tingling at the influx of nicotine. Two cars sat in the lot, his beat-up sedan from the nineties, barely hanging on with little more than coat hangers, duct tape, and hope. Then there was his boss's car.

The newest Range Rover money could buy, dark green and covered in gaudy gold accents, yet its owner was nowhere to be found. How the owner of a neighborhood convenience store could afford it, Trey wondered about that often. Usually the question was answered by a quick glance at the overpriced cans of ravioli, listed at four dollars each, and imagining just how bad the rest of the prices must be.

"Who the hell would pay four dollars for ravioli?" Trey muttered to the storm.

A flash of lightning cracked overhead and sent a jolt through him.

"Probably the rich folk passing through that find us 'oh so quaint,'" Veronica's voice startled him a second time.

The tall redhead had a habit of scaring him. Somehow, she opened the back door silently every time, subduing the rusted hinges into silence in her efforts to make him jump.

"Jesus." Trey let out a breath he hadn't realized was being held. "Do you have to sneak up on me every time I go for a smoke?"

Veronica gave him that same disarming smile that caught his eye the first day she started there a year ago. Her green button-up clung to her thin frame in the moist air, black skinny jeans showed the subtle curve of her hips. A painfully bright and colorful scarf sat around her neck, tied in the same simple knot as always. It was eccentric at minimum, covered in intricate designs of yellows and greens, forming pink-bordered flowers and trees, dotted with the occasional bird, all on a background of even brighter red that faded to orange near the ends. She said it reminded her of a forest sunset, though Trey only got a headache when he tried to make sense of all the swirls that bound each design to the next.

"Of course silly. What am I supposed to do if I don't scare you?" She leaned down and gave him a kiss on the cheek.

Veronica stood an easy six inches taller than him, something that pushed him away from her in the beginning, but Trey had come to like her height. Being five foot six, having a six-foot girlfriend came in handy. Screw what anyone in town thought, he didn't have to jump to reach things anymore.

Trey snuck a subtle hand behind her neck as she leaned back, and pulled her in for a real kiss. Her smile against his lips sent his heart pounding harder than any scare.

Veronica stood up. "Come on, Hector's coming back soon and I don't want to hear him yell at you again."

Trey groaned and stuck his hands in his pockets. "Come on, this place sucks. When are we gonna just disappear and leave him to run his own store?"

She shrugged and looked over him at the podunk town. "I like it here. It's home."

"Esperville? Come on, there's a whole world out there!" Trey grinned. "One waiting for us to explore it."

Veronica gave a wicked smirk. "You mean for me to describe as you stand on your toes trying to see over the fence?"

Trey sputtered at the unexpected quip.

Veronica laughed, bright smile flashing in the gray light. "Get to work, and maybe I'll consider letting you sit on my shoulders as we explore the world."

"H-hey! I'm not *that* short!" Trey chased her through the back door.

The cramped store room was packed with boxes that wilted in the damp air, long abandoned displays, and quickly deteriorating boxes of fresh stock. Cat litter was scattered across the cracked concrete floor to soak up intruding water that ran through every crack in the walls, creating a slick, pasty mess.

"I don't know, you look pretty short from up here," Veronica giggled as she expertly maneuvered around the debris to the main door.

The pair burst into the store, raucous laughter erupting from them as Trey tackled her. They fell in a heap to the floor, out of breath.

Veronica patted his head. "At least you're quick."

Trey gave a playful glare. "Y'know, if I could reach the high shelves, you'd be in trouble."

She planted a distractingly tender kiss on his lips. "Good thing you can't then."

Someone cleared their throat from a nearby aisle.

"Shit, customer." Trey struggled to untangle from Veronica and leapt to his feet. "Sorry about that, how can I... oh no."

"Trey. Veronica." The store owner, Hector, raised an eyebrow at their display. "I see you're making good use of the time I pay you for."

Veronica heaved in a deep breath and stood. "Sorry Hector. Things were quiet and we got a bit bored."

The owner shook his head. "I'll be generous and assume it was merely an hour you two took, instead of docking the full day's pay. Consider that a warning."

Trey bristled at his words. "What?"

The store around them was devoid of life. Fully stocked shelves and t-shirt racks, a world of color somehow devoid of warmth. Hector had that effect everywhere he went.

The town barbecue shut down three hours early when he showed up and started lecturing anyone nearby about the dangers of supermarkets to small towns.

Hector fixed Trey with his usual no-nonsense stare, brown eyes lifeless and bland. "A day it is then, mister Black."

Trey's heart fell. "No, wait. I need the hours. We were just-"

"Just using my valuable store as a playground. You can earn some of the time back by staying late to clean the backroom." Hector ran a hand through his black, slicked back hair. The tan suit jacket shifted like a solid piece, raising the question of just how much starch the stickler used to keep himself so statuesque.

Oh, I'll clean something. Trey's shoulders tensed as he readied another rebuttal.

"I'll help," Veronica's hand rested on his shoulder, melting the tension, "If that's okay?"

Hector gave a curt nod. "Fine, it'll take less time that way."

With the final comment Hector turned and strode from the store, dress shoes clacking loudly with every step.

"I'm gonna cut your pay," Trey mocked as the door closed.

Veronica let out a low chortle. "Not even gonna wait for the door to close? You're an idiot."

"Hey, you chose me." Trey shrugged and leaned against the counter. Veronica just shook her head and began walking to the aisles, inspecting the unchanged items.

"Fine, I'll get started in the back since you're up here anyway." Trey stole a final look at Veronica's ass before disappearing through the door.

The stench of wet cardboard assaulted his nostrils once again, mixed with the acrid burn of too much cat litter.

Ugh, there's a reason I hold my breath through here. A sharp kick sent a ball of soaked litter scattering across the floor.

Bits of the clumps splashed through the small rivers of water that ran from the walls towards the clogged drain in the center of the room. Gray water bubbled occasionally as the pressure built then released through the blockage before another clump clogged it once again.

"For such a fancy dude, he really just lets this place go to hell." Trey grabbed the broom from beside the door.

The bristles stayed stuck to the floor, cemented in place and pulling the head free of the handle.

Trey let out a sigh. "It's been about five minutes. Sounds like time for another smoke break."

He stuck his head into the shop proper. "Hey, Veronica?"

A muffled response came from the clothing rack she was reorganizing yet again.

"I'm just gonna assume you asked me what I want. I'mma head out back again, if you wanna join me? I'm sure captain dick won't be back again for at least an hour."

Veronica popped upright, her hair a mess. "Already? What'd you break?"

Trey rolled his eyes. "Nothing! Just, the broom, kinda, came apart," he mumbled.

"Seriously?"

Trey shrugged. "C'mon. Didn't you say something about some new flowers or somethin' behind the trash cans? Show me."

Veronica smirked and shook her head. "I knew you were waiting to use that against me." She playfully shouldered her way past him. "Come on then, since you're only going to look because it means you can procrastinate."

Trey wrapped an arm around her waist and pulled her back with a laugh. "No, now I'm procrastinating."

Veronica slipped from his grasp. "Uh huh. Let's go look at flowers, lover boy."

Trey followed, smiling to himself as he watched Veronica walk ahead of him. "You know you love me."

A small chuckle escaped Veronica as she kept walking without a word.

Trey raised an eyebrow, his smile faltering. "Right?"

Veronica stopped at the corner of the fenced in trash cans. "You can't be short and insecure." She gave him a taunting smile. "But yes, I do." She took his hand and pulled him around the fence.

A group of glowing, bright flowers filled what was once a small patch of grass. Even in the gloomy gray of the storm, the blooms were near blinding, shining orange blossoms tinted with gold.

"Woah." His attention was immediately captivated by the plants. "Those are insane."

Veronica gave his hand a squeeze, her voice low, "I told you."

He leaned down, examining the flowers. Dark stems rose from the muddy earth, a tangle of vines and woody thorns. The orange of flowers grew brighter the closer he got, the golden flecks and edges reflecting an orange sunlight that was not present in the sky above.

"What are they reflecting?" Trey mumbled the question as Veronica knelt down next to him.

"No idea. But I really want to take a clipping and grow some." She put a hand on his back.

"Yeah...." He leaned in closer, examining a larger fleck of gold.

The reflected sky was orange and dusty looking. Tan clouds swirled overhead, shadows dancing precariously as some unseen thing moved.

"What is that?" He leaned closer, drawn in by the movements.

"Don't," Veronica warned, "we don't know if they're poisonous."

"Yeah... I'll be careful." Trey gently brushed a finger against the stem, avoiding the thorns. "It almost feels warm."

"That's weird." Veronica followed his lead, prodding at the stem.

"Come here." Trey stood up again and set one foot in the patch, careful to avoid stepping on another the flowers themselves. "There's a thin bit here."

"What part of 'they might be poison' did you miss?" Veronica's hands settled on her hips.

Trey shrugged. "It's fine, just move slow and don't get poked." He gave his trademark stupid grin.

Veronica rolled her eyes. "Why would I want to risk that?"

Trey reached for her hand. "The opportunity for an amazing picture with me."

Veronica sighed, giving in to his insistence. "One picture, then back to work. Hector's gonna dock you a week at this rate."

Trey held her hand, offering support as she stepped into the small clearing with him. He pulled out his phone, raising it as high as possible to get the flowers and their faces in frame.

"Give it." Veronica took the phone from him, raising it to the full height of her arm.

"That's so not fair." Trey squeezed her waist. "But somehow, it's kinda hot too."

Veronica rolled her eyes. "Look at the camera, lover boy." She smiled and took the picture.

The flash went off, blinding Trey. The bright light was joined by the sudden sensation of falling, like the world had given way directly beneath him. The soggy mud no longer sucking his feet down, just empty air, then sliding.

Trey screamed as his feet fell out from under him like they were on ice. A heavy thump rumbled through Trey as he hit the ground, scorching sand splashing up like water from the impact.

"Ow," he wheezed, the breath knocked from his lungs.

Veronica's startled cry rang in his ears before she thumped into the ground next to him.

Trey forced himself onto his elbows, skin burning on the sand, and looked to his girlfriend. "You okay?"

Veronica sucked in a sharp breath. "Can't ... breathe...."

Trey rolled her on her side and rubbed her back. "What happened?"

He gazed around. The stormy day was replaced with a scorchingly hot one, the gray sky now filled with tan clouds and dust that covered a deep orange sunlight. The small town was now desert covered, seemingly abandoned and sand blasted.

"Where the fuck are we?" The words barely tumbled from his lips as his mouth went dry.

Veronica took another, deeper breath, coughing into the sand. Her eyes went wide and searched the surrounding area. "W-what the fuck?"

Trey shook his head. "No idea."

The sun above was already cooking them and forced their breathing into short gasps of the scalding air.

"We gotta get inside." Trey looked back to where the convenience store stood. It was now dilapidated and sagged into the desert below. The look of it felt dated, far older than he or Veronica were.

"I'm not going in there." Veronica shook her head. "We should stay here. It's probably some hallucination, flowers can do that sometimes...."

Trey shakily made it to his knees. "Even if it is, that means we're sitting in the mud and rain. Come on."

Veronica looked between him and the dated market, and back again. "Fine."

Trey stood and offered his hand. He froze when Veronica let out a blood curdling shriek as she tried to stand.

"Ow! Ow, ow, ow." She pointed to her leg. The patch of flowers remained where they had been before, though her leg was stuck in the thick of it. Thorns tore through the fabric of her jeans. The woody stems dug deep into her flesh, Seeming to almost draw out the blood from her leg.

"Okay, deep breath." Trey looped a hand under her shoe, the other under her knee above the flowers.

"No, please don't. Just give me-" Veronica's words devolved into a sharp screech as he yanked her leg free in one motion.

"Sorry." Trey set her leg away from the flowers. "We don't know if they're dangerous, I couldn't leave you there." He brushed sweat drenched hair from her eyes.

Veronica stifled a sob and nodded. "Mhm." She gritted her teeth, lips little more than a tight, white line across her face.

"Come on, you can lean on me." Trey pulled her up, standing on the side of her injured leg.

The pair hobbled to the slightly open door. A small pile of sand had blown in, creating a ramp down to the tile floor.

"What is this place?" Trey glanced around, finding aged boxes of worn food packaging of brands he'd never heard of.

"I don't know, I just wanna sit." Veronica moaned, hopping on one leg, braced on Trey's shoulder.

"Oh, right, sorry." Trey helped her into the store proper. past the store room door they found the store opened up into more of a small supermarket than the previous convenience store. The building seemed to have been expanded at some point, allowing for multiple aisles and sections. The shelves stood mostly empty aside from worn cans and torn open boxes, whatever was once inside now little more than piles of dust. To the side of the door was a bench, where Trey helped Veronica sit.

She took in a sharp breath in, settled onto the bench, and reached down to inspect her leg. "Jesus that hurts."

Trey knelt next to her. The flesh on her calf was already bright red and seeping blood from multiple punctures.

"That doesn't look good. I'm gonna look and see if there's a pharmacy."

Veronica grabbed his wrist. "Please don't leave me." Fear wavered in her voice. "Something happened, I don't know what, but this can't be home. It can't be." Tears pricked at the edges of her eyes.

Trey patted her hand. "The place is abandoned. I'll stay in ear shot. I promise. But we can't just ignore this. Wound first, figure out where we are second."

Veronica shook her head slightly before nodding. "O-okay."

Trey padded through the store along the back wall. The shelving sagged and was torn down in areas. Empty cans littered the floor, damaged tiles cracked and popped underfoot. The scent of dust and heat filled the air. Even inside, it was easily ninety.

Trey covered his mouth. "Pretty sure those tiles are asbestos." He coughed a little, lungs feeling itchy.

He kicked a cart, the wheels screeching their protest as it shuddered away.

"What was that?" Veronica's voice echoed from a few aisles down.

"Just me, I kicked a cart." Trey called back, meandering further into the store.

"Please don't do that again." She called back.

"Can do." He muttered, attention drawn to the changed store once again.

As much as anxiety tugged at his mind, curiosity at their predicament stayed in the forefront.

How the fuck did we get here? Hell, where is here?

Trey looked to the dilapidated signs above him, the directory dust coated and hard to read. He squinted at it, unable to find the pharmacy.

"Damn it." He kicked an empty can, and idea springing to mind.

Dust showered from the sign as the can clanged against it and skittered off into another aisle.

"Fuck yeah." Trey raised a fist in the air. "Trey one, weird-ass desert zero."

A short scream from across the store rang in his ears. "Sorry!"

He waited to hear back, though there was no response. *Great, now she's gonna be mad at me too.*

He refocused on the sign. The pharmacy was only two aisles further. "Okay, here we go."

Behind the counter smelled of aged rot as he entered, the meds still sealed and a mummified corpse slumped against one of the shelving units.

Trey frowned at it. "That's not a hopeful sign."

The corpse drew a sense of familiarity. Dust covered, yet perfect, dress shoes, pair of expensive slacks, and a suit jacket starched near into stone.

Holy shit. I wished you'd keel over a few times, but I never meant it. Trey knelt next to Hector's mummified corpse.

Hector was curled up against the shelving, knees pulled to his chest. His once anger filled face now gaunt and dry, teeth dry and cracked, eyes long removed by some pest and leaving a truly dead stare behind.

I guess, somehow, we are still 'home'. But what version of home is this? Trey glanced over the counter, the front glass of the store still facing main street. The asphalt couldn't be seen through the feet of sand piled over it. Street lamps hung precariously, most of them already fallen and half buried.

Anxiety overtook his curiosity, threatening to send him sprinting back to Veronica. "Breathe. She still needs meds."

Trey took a deep breath and stood. He searched the bottles above, glaring at the long medicinal names on each one. "How the hell am I supposed to know what's what?"

Trey angrily tossed a bottle. It rattled and shook another shelf where paper bags vibrated their distaste at the disturbance.

His eyes widened. "Now that's helpful."

Trey tore through the worn paper of one after another, searching the prescriptions for anything involving infection or antibiotics, even something for inflammation would do. Fifteen bags later, and he had three bottles. A painkiller, an antibiotic, and something that claimed to help with swelling.

He jogged from the pharmacy back to where he left Veronica. "Hey I-"

Trey slid to a stop in the dust. The bench had a clean spot on it where Veronica had been sat, little droplets of blood on the ground around it. A trail of red specks lead down the near aisle.

"Veronica?" He whispered to the empty spot.

Trey looked down, gaze following the fresh blood trail that led toward the front of the store.

Trey set the bottles down and crept along the trail. Veronica's shuffling footsteps left a gouged trail through the dirt and debris, pocked by drops of red. Hand prints broke the dust on the shelves where she'd leaned for support.

Please be okay. He silently prayed.

Trey slunk to the end of the aisle, met by a wall of windows just past the registers. Large posters displayed sales and BOGO deals. Most were sun-bleached or torn, the once vibrant colors now dull against the worn ghost town outside. Streams of sunlight streamed between each decrepit advertisement.

The blood trail continued past them and turned toward the door. Trey crouched low to follow the trail, afraid of whatever might be in this unexplored world.

Wind and sand blew across the floor from the open door, muddying the trail. "Damn-"

A hand clamped over his mouth and pulled him back behind the register. He tried to scream against it, muffled and barely able to breathe as fingers tightened on his face.

"Shhh," Veronica's shushing was urgent and frightened.

She pointed out the glass door into the desert covered street. A single woman stumbled through the sand, fear evident on her face. A tattered business suit hung from her shoulders, blood streaming down from a deep gash on her forehead. She called out, voice lost to the wind that picked up as the sun sank lower in the sky.

Trey pulled Veronica's hand down, his voice a shaky whisper, "We should go get her. She'll cook out there."

Veronica shook her head. "Not her, that."

Trey followed her pointing more carefully to the strip of businesses behind the woman. The windows were blown out, the interior filled with shadows. Something darker slunk alongside the woman. Its form was lost to the darkness, leaving only the vague idea of its deer sized body.

"What the fuck?" Trey leaned forward.

"I don't know." Veronica kept a hold on Trey's shoulder. "I heard her yell and wanted to see what was happening. She's been wandering the street the whole time, just back and forth. I think she hit her head; she seems confused."

Trey looked beyond the woman again. "That thing is following her."

Veronica gave his shoulder a squeeze. "There's nothing we can do. I don't know what that is, but I don't want to draw its attention."

Trey fought with the pain rising in his chest at the idea of leaving someone to cook in the sun, or be victim to whatever lurked in the shadows.

"I'm going around. I'll make sure they don't see me." Trey lurched from Veronica's grip.

He froze inches from her hands as the woman stopped. The wind calmed enough to hear relief in her voice, the words still unintelligible. Trey peaked out the door again to see her looking in the window of the building. A man's face floated against the shadows.

Trey shuddered as he studied it. Something about the face sent ice through his veins. The features were too large, too angular, and the mouth just felt wrong.

"What is...." Trey gasped as the mouth opened far too wide It was just human enough to draw the confused in close enough to strike.

The woman shrieked as the form leapt out at her. Dark skin seemed to draw the shadows out with it, large paws ending it two sharp talons smashed the woman to the ground and dug into her shoulders. Her scream ended abruptly as the creature tore into her throat.

Blood curdling cries echoed down the street as more of the creatures emerged. One, two, three, five, seven of them joining the first in devouring the gurgling woman.

"Holy shit." The words tumbled from Trey's mouth, just a little too loud.

One of the creatures perked its head up, this one with the face of a woman, and searched for the source of the noise.

Veronica slapped her hand back over his mouth and yanked him under the register.

The creature strode up to the door and peered inside. It sniffed the air, gaze lazily drifting around the store. With a short huff it leaned against the door frame, the metal groaning under the strain, and scratched itself on it. A disquieting purr vibrated the air as it did so, toes curling into the sand.

Trey fought to keep still, muscles straining as fear coursed through his veins like magma. Veronica's fingers curled harder into his face, nails digging into his cheek as the pair shrunk further under the register, barely able to peer around the counter wall at the beast.

They sat like that for what felt like hours, trying not to so much as breathe as the creature turned and scratched its other side on the metal door frame.

After a few agonizing minutes, the creature huffed and left, disappearing around the corner of the store. Veronica finally released Trey's mouth.

"Holy shit, what the fuck was that?" Trey word vomited in a harsh whisper.

Veronica shook her head, unable to speak, tears streaming down her fearful face.

"We need to get the fuck out of here." Trey extracted himself from under the counter and offered Veronica a hand.

"And go where?"

Trey thought for a moment, mind still reeling and focused on the memory of the creature.

Veronica shook her head. "They're not in here. We should close the doors and keep it that way. There's nowhere to go, not with my leg like this."

Trey opened his mouth to argue, finding himself at a loss for words.

"You know I'm right. We'll just wind up like... her."

Trey looked back out the front. The creatures were gone, only a dark pool of blood left to soak into the sand remained of the woman. Even the bones were gone.

"Yeah." Trey shuddered. "I... I guess you're right."

He offered Veronica his hand again. "I guess at least we have some supplies here. I got you some meds."

Veronica gave a slight nod, keeping her gaze anywhere but out the front door. "Thanks."

Trey helped Veronica toward the back of the store. They shuffled down the aisle, careful to avoid making too much noise.

"Come on, let's stay back here." Trey continued past the bench when Veronica tried to break free of his grasp.

"The back room?" She steadied herself once again on his shoulder. He shrugged. "No windows back their, it seems safer."

Veronica nodded and followed his lead, stifling soft whimpers with every step on her injured leg.

The rest of the evening was silent. Even the wind calmed down to little more than ominous whispering against the edges of the building. Trey found a usable shovel in one aisle and used it to dig the sand out around the doors before closing them. The locks were worn and loose, offering little protection, but it was something.

"Hey." He fell into the makeshift bed next to Veronica, the aged blankets sending out a puff of dust as he did.

She coughed and waved a hand in front of her face. "Thanks for that."

"Yeah, sorry." Trey shrugged and pulled his knees to his chest. "The meds helping at all?"

Veronica nodded. "Yeah, swelling is down, and it doesn't hurt so bad." She planted a kiss on his sweaty, dust covered cheek. "Thank you."

Trey looped an arm around her. They had made their makeshift home in the back room away from sight. The occasional creak of the building made them freeze, not so much as breathing until they were sure it wasn't another creature.

"What are we gonna do?" Trey mumbled to the room.

Veronica shrugged and leaned into his touch, resting her head on his shoulder. "I just wanted to show you pretty flowers."

The wavering crack in her voice brought a lump to Trey's throat.

Stupid. Stupid, stupid, stupid. I had to go and push for a picture, should've stayed back and just looked with her. We could have been home, watching TV, plotting our escape. Instead we're here.

Veronica nuzzled into his shoulder. "Thank you for not leaving me alone."

Trey laid his head on hers. "Even in this fucked up nightmare, I wouldn't dare."

The pair fell into a restless sleep. Nightmares of the creatures plagued their dreams. Trey woke up to Veronica tossing and turning, fearful whimpers escaping her lips.

"Hey, hey. It's okay." He pulled her close, running his fingers through her hair.

Veronica calmed at his touch, though the fear was still evident on her face. He stayed up for the rest of the night, her head on his leg, and listened. Every so often he could hear something scratching at the ceiling above them, followed by quiet caws.

What's up there? Trey wondered. *Maybe it's just an actual bird. Just a normal, every day cr-*

A sharp screech tore through the building, followed by the thump of something heavy hitting the roof. Dust fell in a shower on the pair as Trey leaned over to protect Veronica's face and keep her quiet.

Her eyes shot open, a silent scream dying in her throat as the beating of massive wings dissipated into the distance.

Normal bird zero, desert fuckers one. Trey thought, fighting to keep himself calm.

Veronica's frightened eyes met his, tears pricking at the edges. "We're going to die here."

Trey shushed her quietly. "No, no. I'll find us a way home. Maybe those flowers go both ways."

Veronica shook her head violently. "No, I'm not going near them again. Please, don't make me. Please no." Her words devolved into sobs.

"Okay." Trey brushed her hair again. "It's okay."

Veronica calmed some, sobs quieting into quiet gasps. "Thank you." She buried her face in his stomach.

Trey rubbed her back, calming her back into a somewhat less fitful sleep.

He sighed and leaned back against the wall. His eyes drifted closed, mind returning to the nightmares of a dreamworld instead of the hellscape that awaited them just a precious few inches on concrete away.

Movement woke Trey. Sunlight streamed in from around the door to the main market. Veronica sat up and stretched.

"Sorry, I didn't mean to wake you." She whispered, still half asleep.

"It's okay." Trey rubbed his face, crusted dirt crumbling in a dusty shower into his lap.

Veronica gazed around, eyes bleary and unfocused. "I was hoping it was just a nightmare."

Trey stood slowly, body aching from a night on the floor. "Yeah, me too." He knelt down next to her. "How's the leg?"

Veronica slid the blanket from over her calf and pulled away the blood-stained remains of her pant leg. Bright red veins crawled from every puncture, spreading outward like diseased worms into the healthy flesh of her leg.

"Not good." She winced.

Trey shook his head. "We need to get out of here and get you to a hospital. I can't think of any other way out, the flowers have to be able to do-"

Veronica glared hard at him, her voice unexpectedly throaty and rumbling, "I said no flowers."

Trey froze, unsure whether to comfort her, or run.

Veronica's gaze lightened, then turned to fear. "What's wrong with me?"

Trey gingerly held out a hand to her. "It's okay. Just... I don't know but we'll figure something out."

Veronica shrugged, her skin pale even in the shadowed store room, made more so by the still bright scarf around her neck. "What if you just leave me here? Get yourself out and live."

"What? No, no way am I leaving you here. "He grabbed her shoulder. "Keep taking the meds. I'm gonna find us some cans of food and I'll be right back."

She gave a shaking nod. "Please hurry."

Trey helped Veronica lie back down before stalking out to the market area. He held the shovel like a weapon, poised over his shoulder and ready to swing.

The front door remained closed as sand piled up against it, creating more of a barrier to it opening.

"Okay," he whispered to himself, "At least that's helping."

Every aisle seemed empty, or the few items left were rotting in the heat. Boxes of pasta torn open and strewn into the sand, cans punctured and foaming black sludge out onto the shelves. Even the dry pet food was little more than crumbled dust in cracking, aged bags.

"Fuck." Trey threw yet another rotten can of some unidentifiable sludge down the aisle.

He grabbed the can behind it and gave it a shake. The contents sloshed, but didn't feel as thick as every other can he'd found. A quick inspection revealed it to be in tact, black type print on the can said fruit salad.

"Yes." Trey kept his voice low, heart leaping at the find. "Got Veronica something. Now for me."

He slipped the can into his pocket and continued searching the aisles. Hours later and Trey had one full can of dog food to go along with the fruit salad.

"Gross." Trey shrugged. "But edible."

Trey's stomach rumbled. It had only been a day since they arrived in the desert world, yet going from three meals a day and snacking whenever he wanted, to nothing but hot sand and scalding wind left him wanting and empty.

"Water," Trey mumbled, tongue fat and dry in his mouth. "We need water too."

He picked up a few empty cans and checked the inside for signs of rot. *Okay, got something to put it in, now the question is where do I get water?* He looked up.

The tiled drop ceiling high above was missing most of its pieces. Above that were wires and pipes running in all directions. The lowest pipe had multiple offshoots that connected to fire sprinklers.

Water pipes, obviously. Trey smiled at the idea.

He trod along the aisles, gaze locked upward as he followed the pipes to the wall where they disappeared. Eye level on the wall was a fire control box. Trey slid the handle of the shovel through the metal loop and leveraged it open.

A low groan echoed from the metal before it popped and squealed open, the hinges shrieking in protest to the movement. Inside was the main control valve for the system, and a purge valve that would dump straight onto the floor in case the system ever over-pressurized.

"Now, I wonder if the desert has people working in the pump station." Trey looked over the large wheel in front of him. The center of its spoked frame was held in place by a rusted in place nut. Regardless, Trey grabbed the wheel and yanked on it, dragging himself across the dust covered tiles.

"Fuckin' thing." Trey glared at the frozen valve. "Just turn and let me drink damnit."

He jammed the shovel handle between the spokes and gave it a test pull. The wood held firm, offering another chance at turning the valve. Trey braced his feet against the base of a nearby shelf and leaned back, pulling with his entire body. A low groan emitted from the wheel before it popped free. The sudden spin sent Trey stumbling back into the shelving.

A grumble came from somewhere beneath the ground, followed by burbling and banging as the pipes accepted whatever liquid came from below.

"Hell yeah!" Trey shot a fist in the air as the pipes shook. "Come on baby, give it here."

Another grumble from the pipes before the blow off valve cracked and shot off, reddish brown water spraying across the floor. Walls of mud built up into a channel around the stream of water as it cascaded across the aisle.

"Oh shit." Trey scrambled to get the cans ready, unsure of how long the water would run for.

He stood by the deluge, watching intently as the muddy liquid slowly turned tan, then white with pressure. He quickly filled three cans, then yanked on the shovel, closing the valve. The rush of water trickled to a stop.

Trey grabbed the three cans, peering at the clear liquid inside. He gave it a sniff, then a sip. The cool water soaked into his parched tongue, leaving a taste of damp earth with a slight metallic tang to it.

Trey shook his head and took another swig. "Better than nothing I guess."

He made his way back to the store room, giving another cursory glance along the aisles as he did so. Nothing changed, despite his hopes for a better meal.

The door to the store room opened quietly, the hinges in surprisingly good condition compared the rest of the store. He peered in, met by the sight of Veronica's once again sleeping form. A gentle nudge to her shoulder only elicited a quiet snore.

"Rest up baby." Trey looked down her body to the injured leg.

In the time it took him to find any food, it almost looked like the dark veins had stretched further out, nearly wrapping around her entire calf.

"What the hell was in those flowers?" His heart ached for her, worry flooding his thoughts.

I have to get her home. Why doesn't she want to go near the flowers again? I know they hurt, but still. The image of her absolute horror, and anger, at the idea of nearing the plants flashed in his mind. *Maybe there's some sleeping pills in the pharmacy. I don't want to, but if she won't come willingly... and she needs help.*

Trey settled on the plan, ignoring the knot that formed in his stomach at the idea. He pulled the pop tab on the fruit salad and opened it, sneaking a sip of the sugary syrup inside. The fresh taste coated his tongue in a euphoric moment.

"Fuck that's good."

Veronica rolled over, eyes drooping with sleep. "What is?"

Trey gave her a half smile and handed over the can. "Here, I just tested to make sure it wasn't rotten like everything else."

Veronica smiled at the gesture and took the can, peering down inside it. "Fruit salad?" She gave him a wider smile. "You found my favorite in a nightmare realm. My knight in shining armor."

Veronica's hand gently patted Trey's face. Her skin was icy, even in the sweltering store.

Trey kept his face calm, forcing a smile at the gesture as more panic rose like bile in his throat. "That's me. Now eat."

Trey pulled out his can of dog food, pulling off the top. He grimaced at the pate inside, fighting down a gag at the idea of eating it.

"What'd you get? Rot?" Veronica raised an eyebrow.

"Worse, dog food."

Veronica let a sad smile cross her face. "Come on Romeo, I'll split the fruit with you, give me half the dog food."

Trey scooted back. "No way, you have plenty worse to worry about. I'll make do with my... mystery meat."

Veronica shook her head. "I'm only eating half of this; the rest will go to waste otherwise."

Trey's shoulders deflated. He knew she would die on this hill if that's what it took for him to eat something real.

"Fine."

Veronica perked up a little, her slumped shoulders rising a bit. Her face remained pale, eyes bloodshot.

How did I miss how bad she looks? Trey fought to keep his face even.

"I look pretty bad if you're looking at me like that." Veronica looked down at her lap. "I'm uh... I don't think I'm getting out of here, am I?"

Agony shot through Trey's chest like a bullet, every word firing another shot into him. "Hey, don't talk like that. I'm getting you out, and help."

Veronica shrugged. "We don't know how we even got here."

"Those damn flowers, that's how. And that's how we'll get out."

Veronica's face went from exhaustion, to pain, then rage. Fear coursed through Trey at the sudden change in her demeanor as her voice came out in a low rumble, "I will not be going near those damned things again."

"Veronica, please. I know they hurt but-"

"No." The finality of her tone silenced him.

Trey nodded and poked at the dog food in his can. "Okay."

Veronica looked up at him. The rage on her face was betrayed by the fear in her eyes. "Please. Just leave me here. I don't feel like myself. Please."

Trey shook his head. "I'll help you. Don't worry. It's just a fever or something, maybe the meds will help it break. I'll go look for more."

Veronica watched him stand, her face calming with every word of agreement he gave. "Thank you. I'm sorry." Tears welled in her eyes, spilling down her dust covered cheeks.

Trey gave a gentle smile, hiding the fear in his mind. *I need to get her out of here now. She's cracking.*

Trey wandered the store for a while, trying to think of any solution better than drugging and carrying Veronica out of the store. Try as he might, nothing else seemed possible.

"They'll just think I'm insane and probably killed her if I go back alone." The idea of convincing paramedics to enter a small circle of flowers that would transport them to another world sounded as insane as he felt.

Eventually, after failing to find anything useful, Trey arrived at the pharmacy. Once again, he dug through the bagged meds until a bottle of sleeping pills tumbled onto the counter.

"Perfect." Trey mumbled. "Now I can feel like an asshole frat boy trying to get laid."

He rolled his eyes, fighting down the disgust at his planned actions boil in his stomach. "Calm down Trey. It's to help her, not hurt her."

Dust and broken bits of tile crunched underfoot with every step. Trey slowed as the storeroom got nearer, uncertain if he could keep his deception hidden. *Hopefully she's asleep again and I can just mix the powder into the fruit salad. Maybe the dog food too, just to be sure. I need a way to separate the two.*

Trey glanced around, his eyes settling on a shelf with a few in tact plates on it. He wiped the dust off one with his shirt. Light streaks of grime remained behind.

"Better than it was." He whispered, grabbed another, and carried his find to the store room.

Veronica was asleep again, fitfully tossing and turning, her face screwed up into a grimace.

Trey moved to her, checking her leg once more. The red veins, now darker and inflamed, snaked around the calf entirely now, reaching up towards her knee and disappearing under the jeans.

He could swear the lines were now shifting and writhing under the light that streamed in from the store front. Trey shook his head. *Maybe I'm the one that's cracking now.*

He grabbed the untouched can of fruit salad from her side and dumped half of it on the plate. The syrup mixed with the dust into a brown sludge.

Okay, that's mine then. Trey cracked open two capsules and dumped them into the can, giving it a swirl to dissolve the first capsule. He followed the same with the dog, food, plopping his half on the plate and mashing hers up with the other capsule's contents.

Trey gave her shoulder a squeeze. "Hey, Veronica."

She stirred, eyes fluttering open to reveal glazed over orbs. "Hm? I can't...." She blinked rapidly before the pasty color dissipated. "That's better." She sighed.

He swallowed the knot of fear in his throat that formed with the sight of her eyes. "You didn't eat. come on." Trey pulled her up to a sitting position. "Here." He handed her the two cans.

She took them, tipping the can of fruit to her lips. Her stomach twitched, a gag erupting from her throat as the sweet syrup sprayed around her face. Veronica coughed and dropped the can, spilling its contents. "Ugh, that was absolutely rotten." She wiped her mouth.

"What?" Trey took a piece of fruit from his plate and bit into it. The sickly-sweet syrup once again coated his mouth, grainy with sand, the fruit bland and flavorless. "No, it's definitely not rotten."

Veronica shook her head. "Fine, you get sick. I'll just stick to, uh, this." She sniffed at the can of dog food.

Trey froze as her single sniff turned into a deep inhale before Veronica snatched a handful of the meat sludge and shoved it into her mouth. Disgusting smacking and chewing sounds erupted from her, along with grunts of satisfaction as she dug more of the dog food from its tin.

"Uh, Veronica?"

She ignored his words, smacking and slurping bits off her fingers.

"Veronica." Trey said a bit louder.

She looked at him, finger in her mouth. The ravenous woman gave a sheepish grin. "Sorry. It's just really good. Try it."

Trey picked a small bit off the chunk of pink mush on his plate, placing it on his tongue to Veronica's encouragement. Salty slime coated his tongue in an instant, followed by a powerfully sour aftertaste of unknown and mixed meats. Trey fought down a gag.

"Baby that fever has gone to your head." Trey said, holding his tongue out of his mouth.

"Fine, give it to me then." Veronica held out an eager hand, nearly shaking with anticipation.

"All yours." Trey held out the plate, and watched it horror as she scarfed the second half.

Veronica gave a contented sigh and slumped back against the wall. "Mmmm." She smacked her lips loudly.

"Alright then." Trey looked back to he fruit salad on his plate, thoroughly disgusted. "I'm going to, uh, go make sure everything is closed up for the night.

Veronica nodded lazily. "Okay." She closed her eyes, already on the verge of sleep again.

Trey wandered the store for another hour, ensuring Veronica would be fast asleep by the time he returned.

The storeroom was long dark by the time he had the courage to check. His throat was dry with anticipation, nerves alight with fear.

He prodded her shoulder, only to be met with snores. "Hey, you awake?"

No response came from Veronica.

"I'm sorry for this." Trey looped his arms under hers and began dragging her toward the door.

It fought against his pushing, the sand on the other side piled against it.

"Come on." Trey whispered to himself and gave another shove.

Just enough space opened for him to slip through and pull Veronica out into the sand. Even with the sun low on the horizon, heat emanated up from the sands, threatening to cook him if he didn't hurry.

A quick glance around confirmed empty desert outside the store. He looked to the sky, searching for any signs of whatever hit the roof the night before.

"Now's the only chance I'm getting." He hefted Veronica up again, her feet digging two trenches in the sand as he dragged her.

It took far longer to get back to where the flowers grew than he expected. Sweat drenched Trey's clothes, dehydration threatening to make him drop.

"Just. A little. More," Trey panted, groaning with effort at each step.

The orange blossoms glowed in the waning light, their golden edges flashing brightly. The dark stems seemed to wave, drawing him towards them.

"Come on you bastards. Send us home." Trey stood at the edge of the grouping. The golden flecks reflected the blue sky of their hometown, the fence around the trashcans visible in some of them.

"Okay, here we-" Trey was knocked aside viciously, stumbling into the sands.

He caught a glimpse of Veronica stood over him, her leg dark, tendrils of vines reaching from the flowers and digging under her flesh. Small thorns protruded from her skin, more dark lines actively snaking under her skin. Her hands flexed angrily, tendrils rising from the edges of her bright scarf her neck towards her head. Once bloodshot eyes now seemed to pulse with a fury Trey had never seen in her.

Her voice was deep and cracked, more like the sound of branches breaking than speech.

"I said, no flowers."

She reached down to him, her hand wrapping tightly around his wrist.

A bloodcurdling scream escaped Trey's lips as the first of the thorns emerged from her palm, digging their way into his flesh, thin vines snaking through his wrist and up the arm.

Somewhere, Someplace

Junior Sokolov

Corvin arrived at the deserted town of Esperville. Scratch that. Semi-deserted. Some stragglers had refused to leave their homes and businesses after the request for a temporary evacuation came in. Contracted security, along with the National Guard, patrolled the town irregularly for looters and vandals. Corvin was neither. He was a collector and facilitator of collections—clean-cut, young but not too young. Ordinary. Still, wandering around in plain view might attract unwanted attention.

A glance at his watch told him it was only five minutes past seven in the early evening. Soon, it would be fully dark, and sooner, his contact would show up. To pass the time, he pulled up the email app on his smartphone and re-read the message from the collector. He knew her already; she was in his collection. Her message was professional and succinct, with a forwarded thread between her and the artist, and photos attached.

"This piece should be in my collection. I paid for it, but the artist is dead. Can you retrieve it for me? I'll pay you 20% of the original price."

The woman didn't shy away from asking him to retrieve whatever extra pottery he could from the dead potter's home. Appropriate payment would be given per piece, of course.

The problem was...the potter's home was about a mile from where this mess started. The problem was...it lay behind a chain-link fence, followed by a taller and beefier cement enclosure that was, however, still under construction. And armed guards. Don't forget the armed guards. They wouldn't shoot him, but they would still stop him. How to get in? A problem indeed—but he knew collectors who knew collectors. And collectors, well, they were everywhere.

He schmoozed, chatted up his connections, the collectors' sites, the chat rooms, public and private, until he found the one. The one collector who was in the right place at the right time.

Thirty-something Albert Madden held an obsessive love for all types of G.I. dolls. He had rooms full of military dolls, plastic trucks, airplanes, and futuristic vehicles with accessories. But his collection lacked a mint edition of a 1970 G.I. Jack—yes, Jack—from a small company that hadn't lasted as long as a fart in the wind. During their brief existence, they released four types of dolls. Three were lost to history. And the fourth—Albert's current holy grail—Corvin found in the possession of a woman who collected all nurse and nursing memorabilia. She sent it his way in exchange for a 1975, handmade G.I. Nurse doll from the Vietnam era.

He mused again about the lock-and-key relationships between collectors and their collectibles—the items that brought them joy and filled the hollow. He sipped his latte and let his mind wander until, from the corner of his eye, he saw a figure walking up the hill, and he stepped out of the car.

You can't tell a collector's age by what they collect. He had met an old dude who collected the freshest Monster High dolls and young women with a desire for ancient Pez dispensers. The demographic for G.I. Joes toys was men aged forty-five and up, but if Albert was younger than thirty, he'd be amazed. And he was no G.I. or security contractor, with his long curly hair and fresh looks, but otherwise, he looked as average as a man could look. Only his black jeans, black shoes, and dark hoodie made him look a bit shady. Average height and weight, the man held out his hand, but not to shake.

"Hi, I'm Al. Can I see it?"

"Sure thing."

The G.I. Jack changed hands. The figurine lay in its original box, whose cardboard sides were warped from uncaring storage. Its edges were dinged and scuffed, and the colors were faded. Time hadn't been kind to the box. But Al held it with the reverence a medieval monk would have for a reliquary heavy with the bones of a saint. He laid it on the hood of the car, pulled off the lid, and set it aside. Then he began to inspect the box's contents. The tiny folded pamphlet with the bio for the figurine and adventure suggestions came first. He read it with a grin and set that aside too, then he lifted the doll. He ran his fingers over the ill-fitting, stiff clothing, moved the small limbs, and examined the plastic accessories. His fingertips ran over G.I. Jack's face and the faux hair. No plastic hairdo for this doll.

"I can take it now, right?"

"It's all yours."

Al pulled a minimalist nylon backpack from the pouch of his hoodie, smiling like a boy who had just taken the perfect Christmas present from under the tree, and placed the box inside.

"Let's go, then. We'll take my car—they'd take down your license plates. I'll drive us close to the fence, but we'll have to walk the rest of the way. It's not too bad."

Al drove them past the quiet town, all the way into the hills above, from the newly paved roads onto a country road, and parked on the side where trees gave extra privacy. They got out and walked a mile to a spot on the fence where a ladder and a blanket over the barbed wire helped them over with ease.

"How'd you accomplish that?" asked Corvin.

"I'm ashamed, but sticks and carrots. One of them collects vintage beer cans, and I found the one he wanted and bought it for him. The other sleeps with the captain's wife."

"Why the shame?"

He didn't see Al blush but sensed it in his voice and heard him lick his lips before he replied, almost in a whisper.

"Blackmail? I never thought I'd blackmail anybody."

"I can imagine. Go to confession and get absolved with a few hail Marys."

"That's for Catholics."

"Just don't tell the priest you're not, and let him do his magic."

Albert's stifled laugh came out as a snort.

"How dangerous is this?" asked Corvin.

"Not very. The flowers only bloom in the summer, but we're trying to make them bloom year-round—"

"You're a florist?"

This time, the laugh escaped. "I'm a botanist! Jesus Christ, a florist..."

"Just kidding, guy." Corvin grinned. "I find it hard to believe that a field of flowers can take a person to an entirely different dimension. Is it true? Bullshit, right?"

Al was quiet for so long that Corvin figured he'd get nothing more out of him on the subject.

"Anyway, the plants aren't having it. They bloom in the summer, so, no portal to worry about. The army cleared the area of critters as far as I know. All the dangerous ones, anyway. Every once in a while, I see some weird insects. Our only worry is that someone might see us." He paused, and when he resumed, his tone was subdued. "It's a big worry for me. I'd lose my job and get prosecuted."

"We'll be okay."

At the cement wall, they walked until they reached a metal hatch on the side. Al knelt by it, grasped the grid, and with a sharp shove, pushed it in.

"It's bolted from the inside, but I crawled through it this morning and removed the bolts. Duct-taped it there." He ducked to the side and waved Corvin in. "After you—I'll put this back in place once we're in."

***

When they arrived at the potter's house Corvin saw more signs of the future to come. The road had been widened to allow constructions trucks and equipment. Building supplies also rested by the side and large swaths of land had been cleared. He was no tree hugger but seeing his much destruction always hurt. A tap on his shoulder got him back on track.

"Let's hurry up. You've seen how we got in, it's pretty narrow. How much do you think you can take out?"

Corvin shrugged. "Don't know. Anyone in there?" he pointed at the house.

"Not yet, soon. The plan is to turn this entire hill in a scientific, military are. I guess they'll tear it down. I think you want the studio anyway."

They walked quickly to the barn that used to be the potter's studio and froze at the threshold where the swirls of blood and dirt still marred the floor. Corvin wondered about the bodies, but pulled out his smartphone took a few shots and walked in. The place was in parts a mess, in parts as pristine looking as that of any working artists. As he searched for his collectible he found the painted wall at the back. A wild collage created with paint, photos, maps and found objects. A map of a would-be Nevada from another place.

"It's all true," muttered Corvin.

Al snorted. "Hell yeah, it's all true. But for their own good the American public won't hear about it."

"The Ansel documentary got it in the teeth," replied Corvin.

"They paid an agency to discredit t it. Influencer, tabloids...The works. That woman is mighty mad now, but to be fair...she rushed it. That movie was a rush job. Anyway, let's get what you need and go."

Corvin pulled out the duffle bag he'd tucked in the waist band at the back of his jeans. It'd be awkward but it'd fit in that small tunnel if he dragged it behind. Like a dead body, his mind morbidly suggested. He pulled up the gallery on his phone and looked at the images the collector had sent. The piece he'd been expecting could be carried in hand, it wasn't even very big. But having made it all the way in, he wasn't getting out with as much extra loot as he could carry.

His luck held. He found the piece the collector wanted, a strange sculpture. But under the light of the flashlight its reds, rusts and metallic touches beguiled. A pretty piece, he thought as he wrapped it in paper, and placed it in one of the many empty boxes laying around before placing it in the bag. He repeated that operation with any work that looked valuable, portable and collectable. Then he hit something of a jackpot.

"This is a diary." He muttered as he opened a black sketchbook, filled with notes, drawings and photos. He stuffed it in the bag, this would be coming back with him to read at leisure.

***

"Do you really need this?" Al whined as he looked at the camera in Corvin's hands.

"You have your collection; I have mine. No mention of tonight's trade—you've nothing to worry about there."

Al's face twitched, he looked unconvinced but resigned. "This is not how you get to know a person."

"We're not dating, Al," replied Corvin as he took the first photos of Albert Madden and spent the next hour listening to his story, trying to find the reason behind the collections. The why. Everything had a why, he believed. He collected whys and collectors. Al's reticence melted as he talked his way through his collection, introducing pieces, holding them up for inspection—some with the care reserved for newborns. He had many whys, but Corvin thought the main one was losing the brother he'd played with in childhood and his teenage years. A good why, thought Corvin, who would enter photos and text in his own journal, mindful to skip the incriminating details. That would remain in his memory.

He didn't get the call until almost a week after the Esperville retrieval. Collectors knew collectors, and word got around about what came from where—and who got it out. The voice on the phone betrayed the man's age. His diction, the caller's class and education.

"I would like to hire you to bring me back one of the portal blooms."

Corvin winced. "No can do. The first thing the army engineers did was build a greenhouse around them, and even if I could get it out—which I don't believe I can—I've no interest in being the Rosenberg of my era. More important, from everything I've heard, they're a health hazard."

"The Rosenbergs!? Ethel and Julius Rosenberg. Bit dramatic, isn't it? It's at a college. The pathologist sent samples to a college. They remained there. I've spoken with the person who received them, and she confirmed potting them. I'll pay you three thousand in cash just to check if they are there. Six if you bring at least one back to me."

"Money isn't everything."

"You collect collectors, do you not? I'll give you access to my collection and answer any questions you have. I will also owe you a favor, and I always pay my debts."

"Plus, the money."

"Plus the money," the collector agreed, a tone of calm satisfaction in his voice.

Well, why not, Corvin thought. He had tasted the bait and taken the hook.

Damn my curious nature, he thought. But if the powers that be hadn't done their due diligence and secured the college...well, that was their fault, still.

"What do you collect?" Most collectors didn't just collect one thing. Corvin hoped it wasn't some nut with a passion for garden gnomes or vintage boxes of Velveeta cheese.

"High-value cars, old comic books, toys from the '40s through the '60s, and...orchids."

***

Not even a week later, November arrived, chilly but mellow. The fog that early morning was thick, and it was dark, just as Corvin had planned when he set his alarm for 2 a.m. He got back to Esperville after an hour of driving and parked discreetly in an alley not too far from the college. The college's online map had provided clear directions, and after a short walk through the silent streets he found the greenhouse nestled between a tiny student park and two buildings: the old Astoria Hall and the newer Columbia Hall.

At the greenhouse's entrance, he hesitated. His client had told him where the plant would be—way at the back. But during the last two months of summer, whatever was in there had grown wild, its spread checked only by the glass walls of the greenhouse. How in the name of God no one had caught this, he couldn't begin to guess. But wild, bramble-looking things covered the sides of the greenhouse almost to the ceiling. He placed the flashlight on the glass pane and, in the thick of it all, spotted the plants at the back of the building. With a sigh, he cursed his luck. This wasn't going to be easy. That wild mess of Razorweeds had created a gauntlet of thorns around his prize. He liked the excitement, but he wasn't such a damn fool that he'd risk running in, grabbing the plants, and running out. He'd never make it.

There had to be a back entrance. He walked around the building, and when he reached it, he put on a mask, donned gloves, a pair of safety glasses, and a heavy-duty rain jacket, tying the hood tight over his head. Forcing the lock was child's play, and in under a minute, the door to the stock room was open. The space was filled with earthy-smelling bags of soil and compost, along with the more unusual smells of fertilizers and chemicals he couldn't name. More clutter was added by tools, replacement parts, pots, and boxes. Just five feet away was the inner door to the greenhouse, the one that opened right next to the plants he needed.

Corvin shook himself off, stretched his arms, then got on the balls of his feet. He yanked the door open, grabbed the plant, yanked it back, and slammed the door shut. It had overgrown the small pot and looked like it was on its last legs—or rather, roots. It was wilted; a lot of the leaves were brown and dry, and dead ones curled up at the base of the stem had fallen off long ago. He pulled out the combo containers from his backpack, filled the bottom piece with the dark, damp soil, and replanted it. He checked the plant, plucked some of the dead, brown leaves, then capped it with the tall transparent plastic lid.

Fait accompli, he thought with a sigh of relief. But the other plant was right there, waiting, on the other side of the door and within easy reach. Under-promise but over-deliver, yeah. I like that, he thought as he placed the first one in the backpack.

He got ready again. Loosened up, stretched, balanced on the balls of his feet. Then he yanked the door open, stepped in, and grabbed the second plant just as rough vines lashed out like whips and coiled around his wrist. He screamed as they yanked his arm against the doorjamb, his elbow bending painfully while the thorns dug in. With a roar, he pulled himself back and slammed the door on the vines. Shoving his weight against it, he slammed it repeatedly until the vines broke or retreated, leaving him on one side in bloody agony. On the other side, something heavy thudded against the floor, searching for access.

Gasping in pain, Corvin stared at his arm, bloody and bleeding profusely.

"Fuck!" he roared. "Shit, shit, shit! You fuck!"

But he wasn't a man to lose his mind. He stopped the bleeding as best he could and forced himself to calm down, to slow down. Fear and anger go together, and both make you lose control. Cursing through clenched jaws, he grabbed the second plant he'd thrown to the floor and, with shaking hands, repotted it like the first and threw it into the bag. Fighting chills, nausea, and trembling, he looked at the blood and thought: DNA. He could walk out of there as is, but... DNA. Did he want to leave his identity behind? And whatever was in the other room ought to be dead.

He looked around the room. The gardening tools were useless, of course, but there was a small heater in the corner, plastic sheeting, and containers. And would there be? Yes, there it was.

He created a small nest of plastic sheeting, and on the outside of the nest, he placed bags of ammonium nitrate. All that was left for him to do was to put the heater in the middle, plug it in, and turn the heat on high. The heating coils glowed a vivid, fierce orange, and he bolted. He was back at the car, driving out of the alley when he heard the loud boom.

***

The home wasn't a palace, but it was a damn nice place. Too much class and good design for a McMansion, it had the elegance and taste of old money and wise design—perfect for someone who collected expensive cars. Corvin's arm was bandaged up to the elbow, and the collector's sympathy seemed sincere.

"Can I get you a drink, anything?" asked Harry Leeds, showing him to a seat and grimacing as he looked at Corvin's arm. "I'm so sorry you got hurt. I never thought—I didn't think... well, that those things would have been there."

"Yeah, me neither. Live and learn. Here are your plants."

"Do you have insurance? Can I help you?"

Corvin waved aside the offer. "I'm good, Harry."

"So, now it's time for your collection, right?"

"Yup," Corvin replied with a nod and took out a camera.

He photographed Harry Leeds in front of his collections, recording him as he retold his memories—how certain toys brought back memories of his uncles. With his father, they had restored so many cars. When the house tour was done, Harry picked up the plants and walked Corvin to the greenhouse.

"My wife used to grow them; she loved them. They were her absolute favorite flowers."

"She passed away?"

"A long time ago, decades now. But these orchids... when I'm in this room, I feel closer to the memory of her. To her. She must be somewhere, right? Heaven? Another place? I can't believe that someone you love is completely gone. Erased as if they never existed. They must be someplace."

Decades, but the pain in Harry's voice felt fresh. They must be someplace, waiting for a reunion.

Sure, wouldn't that be nice, mused Corvin. Other photos—some black and white, others with that Kodachrome look, colors richly saturated and warm, tinted slightly red by the passing years—were tacked or framed on the wall.

A family standing outside a casino. A young boy wading in an azure pool under an endless blue sky. The woman with the boy again.

"That's..."

"1969, Las Vegas."

He pointed at a young couple holding a baby. "My wife and son. Both dead. Cancer."

Harry donned thick gloves, knelt with arthritic slowness, and pulled the two portal blooms from their containers. With a trowel, he dug a hole in the loam and replanted them in the middle of a large circular planter, wide enough for three bodies to comfortably stand next to each other.

"From what I heard they grow well. In this soil the rhizomes and stoloms should spread out without any problems."

Corvin didn't have to ask. Come the height of summer, when the plants would bloom, if there were enough of them, Harry would be taking a summer trip.

Authors Biographies

Wren Cavanagh

Wren Cavanagh is a writer from the pacific northwest. Her favorite genre to read and write is horror and gruesome stuff. And because we all need a breather from the bloody and the horrid, she also puts out a few upbeat supernatural cat cozies.

***

Stephanie Hoogstad

Stephanie Hoogstad is a born-and-raised Californian who has built her life around the written word. By day, she toils as a contract editor for a medlegal company and a freelance beta reader, and by night—and any moment she can spare—she pursues her lifelong passion of writing speculative fiction. In addition to being the founder of The Writer's Scrap Bin, Stephanie holds a B.A. in English from the University of California, Davis, and an MSc in Creative Writing from the University of Edinburgh. In 2017, her supernatural thriller "Postmortem" was longlisted for the Crime Writer's Association's Margery Allingham Short Story Competition. Her stories "Patient Zero" and "Beautiful Dreamer" were also published in the Darkness Wired and Sick Cruising anthologies, respectively. When she isn't wrapped up in the world of reading and writing, Stephanie can be found knee-deep in paranormal and history shows, Disney, and her three hyperactive dogs—or catching up on the sleep her dogs have kept from her.

You can learn more about Stephanie and her works at www.thewritersscrapbin.com.

***

Shivangi Narain

Shivangi has a keen interest in exploring the world through fiction. A third-culture upbringing and forays into the digital world in her formative years deeply influence her writing, and her works explore themes of cultures, communities, and identities in flux.

***

Wade Newhouse

Wade Newhouse is a Professor of English at William Peace University in Raleigh, NC, where he teaches a wide range of courses including *Creative Writing*, *Storytelling for Gaming*, and *Ghosts and Vampires*. His scholarly writing includes journal articles and book chapters on Civil War literature, the history of Dracula movies, the Friday the 13th franchise, and Doctor Who. His short fiction has appeared in many anthologies and online zines including Love Letters to Poe, HelloHorror, Horror Obsessive, Sci Fi Shorts, and Notch Publishing's *Sick Cruising*. He is also an actor and director in the Raleigh community theatre scene.

***

Henry Snider

For over 25 years, Henry Snider has dedicated his time to helping others tighten their writing through critique groups, classes, lectures, prison prose programs, and high school fiction contests. He co-founded Fiction Foundry (est. 2012) and the award-winning Colorado Springs Fiction Writer's Group (1996-2013). Thirteen years to the month from founding the CSFWG, he retired from the presidency. After a much-needed vacation, he returned to the literary world.

While still reserving enough time to pursue his own fiction aspirations, he continues to be active in the writing community through classes, editing services, and advice. Henry lives in Colorado with his wife, fellow author and editor Hollie Snider, son – poet Josh Snider and numerous neurotic animals, including, of course, Fizzgig, the token black cat.

The editor of this anthology is only too grateful for his constant advice and encouragement.

His most recent work can be found in the anthology In the Woods published by Polymath Press (November 24, 2023)

***

Josh Snider

Josh Snider is a multi-genre author from a family of writers and editors. He has participated in professional writers' groups for his entire life, being the youngest member of his first group, the award-winning Colorado Springs Fiction Writers Group, and a founding member, and former president, of his current group Fiction Foundry. He has a background in poetry and has since moved into prose.

He has been featured in such anthologies as: *Arithmophobia* and *In the Woods*: a Fiction Foundry Anthology.

***

Junior Sokolov

Junior writes in the horror and sci-fi genre, loves bookstores, writing, and moody gray skies over busy metropolises.

Thank you, dear readers

If you made this far, you have our sincere thanks for letting us entertain you. Pass your time or perhaps even tell you something new you hadn't thought of before.

Please consider checking out our other books and keeps us in mind for your future reads.

Did you love *Alt Vegas: Visitations*? Then you should read *Alt Vegas: Nuclear Dreams*[1] by Wren Cavanagh!

[2]

Newlyweds Kyle and Mandy arrive in the quiet town of Esperville, Oregon, ready to build and sell homes, imagining a bright future together. But Esperville hides a dark secret: the land itself seems to swallow its residents whole. Vanished without a trace. At first, Kyle dismisses the town's disturbing history as local superstition—until a close friend is savagely attacked by a nightmarish creature, and Mandy disappears that same night.

Desperate to find her, Kyle teams up with Sam Oswell, a grieving potter haunted by the mysterious disappearance of his own son. Together, they uncover a doorway to "the Alt"—an eerie, alternate dimension where a breaking time loop, traps its inhabitants in a twisted

---

1. https://books2read.com/u/4AMAE0

2. https://books2read.com/u/4AMAE0

version of 1950s Las Vegas replete with creatures, monsters and evolving lifeforms. This world teems with strange life forms, and reality itself is breaking down.

Worse, it is a two-way door, and Kyle soon realizes that the reality of the Alt has already bled into small and quaint Esperville with deadly results.

To rescue Mandy, Kyle must face mind-bending dangers in both dimensions, confronting a ruthless army officer intent on preserving the Alt's deadly cycle. Time is running out, and as the boundaries between worlds crumble, Kyle must risk everything—not only his life, but the fragile balance of reality itself

Read more at nphzone.com.

Also by Wren Cavanagh

Cat Daddies Mysteries
Bits and Pieces
Of Cats and Sea Monsters

Honeycomb
Honeycomb: Lethal Cargo
Honeycomb: Revelation
Honeycomb: Wraith Ship
Honeycomb: Set One

Race the Dead
The Last Flag

Standalone
Alt Vegas: Nuclear Dreams
Alt Vegas: Visitations

Watch for more at nphzone.com.

Also by Stephanie Hoogstad

Darkness Wired
Sick Cruising
Alt Vegas: Visitations

Also by Shivangi Narain

Sick Cruising
Alt Vegas: Visitations

Also by Wade Newhouse

Sick Cruising
Alt Vegas: Visitations

Also by Henry Snider

Darkness Wired
Sick Cruising
Alt Vegas: Visitations

Also by Josh Snider

Alt Vegas: Visitations

Also by Junior Sokolov

Honeycomb
Honeycomb: Lethal Cargo
Honeycomb: Revelation
Honeycomb: Wraith Ship
Honeycomb: Boljelam
Honeycomb: Set One

Standalone
Darkness Wired
Sick Cruising
Alt Vegas: Visitations